"If we can help you, we will. We're... friends."

"I don't know what to say to that," she muttered, stepping away from him as he did the same.

He studied her, those blue eyes a distraction all on their own. Then add the cowboy hat and stubborn jaw and dark stubble...

"You say thanks. That's it."

She shifted on her feet, wholly nonplussed by the effect he had on her. "Fine. Thanks."

He chuckled, slapped her on the shoulder like they were buddies. Yes, she was quite used to that treatment from men.

But then his hand stayed there, gave her shoulder a little squeeze. She assumed that was the sort of sorry-your-sister-died-and-we-found-the-body gesture a man like Jake made.

But his hand...lingered. And Zara didn't have the first rightly clue what to do with that, and when she heard footsteps approaching, she only knew she had to step away from his hand.

THE LOST HART TRIPLET

NICOLE HELM

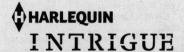

For the savers.

HARLEQUIN®

INTRIGUE™

ISBN-13: 978-1-335-58217-1

The Lost Hart Triplet

Copyright © 2022 by Nicole Helm

All rights reserved. No part of this book may be used or reproduced in
any manner whatsoever without written permission except in the case of
brief quotations embodied in critical articles and reviews.

This is a work of fiction. Names, characters, places and incidents
are either the product of the author's imagination or are used fictitiously.
Any resemblance to actual persons, living or dead, businesses,
companies, events or locales is entirely coincidental.

For questions and comments about the quality of this book,
please contact us at CustomerService@Harlequin.com.

Harlequin Enterprises ULC
22 Adelaide St. West, 41st Floor
Toronto, Ontario M5H 4E3, Canada
www.Harlequin.com

Printed in U.S.A.

Recycling programs
for this product may
not exist in your area.

PLEASE RECYCLE
THIS PRODUCT IS RECYCLABLE

Nicole Helm grew up with her nose in a book and the dream of one day becoming a writer. Luckily, after a few failed career choices, she gets to follow that dream—writing down-to-earth contemporary romance and romantic suspense. From farmers to cowboys, Midwest to *the* West, Nicole writes stories about people finding themselves and finding love in the process. She lives in Missouri with her husband and two sons and dreams of someday owning a barn.

Books by Nicole Helm

Harlequin Intrigue

Covert Cowboy Soldiers

The Lost Hart Triplet

A North Star Novel Series

Summer Stalker
Shot Through the Heart
Mountainside Murder
Cowboy in the Crosshairs
Dodging Bullets in Blue Valley
Undercover Rescue

A Badlands Cops Novel

South Dakota Showdown
Covert Complication
Backcountry Escape
Isolated Threat
Badlands Beware
Close Range Christmas

Carsons & Delaneys: Battle Tested

Wyoming Cowboy Marine
Wyoming Cowboy Sniper
Wyoming Cowboy Ranger
Wyoming Cowboy Bodyguard

Visit the Author Profile page at Harlequin.com.

CAST OF CHARACTERS

Zara Hart—One of the Hart triplets, lifelong resident of Wilde, used to run the Hart Ranch but now works as the ranch hand for the Thompsons since they bought her father out. Determined to prove her sister's innocence.

Jake Thompson—Former navy SEAL and part of Team Breaker, an elite squad of military men who took out terrorist organizations—before a military error made their identities known. They've since been proclaimed "dead" and assigned new identities: the Thompsons, ranching brothers in Wilde, Wyoming, now owners of the Hart Ranch.

Hazeleigh Hart—One of the Hart triplets, occasionally gets premonitions, is arrested for murder when Amberleigh is found dead.

Amberleigh Hart—Hart triplet who went missing ten years ago. Her buried body is found by Zara and Jake on the Hart ranch.

Thomas Hart—A police officer for Bent County Sheriff's Department and the Hart triplets' cousin.

Laurel Delaney-Carson—The detective for the Bent County Sheriff's Department investigating Amberleigh's murder.

Cal, Dunne, Brody, Henry and Landon Thompson—The other members of Team Breaker now living as the Thompson brothers on the Hart Ranch with Jake.

Chapter One

The town of Wilde, Wyoming, was nothing like its name nor its nearest neighbor, Bent, which harbored centuries-old feuds and murderers and kidnappers and the like.

Wilde was small, quiet and *boring.* Aside from *two people* disappearing fifteen years ago which was clearly just a May-December romance leaving judgment behind, and a bank robbery in 1892 that many claimed was fictional, nothing ever happened in Wilde.

Until now.

At least, in Zaraleigh Hart's estimation.

Zara, because no one except her family was allowed to call her Zara*leigh*, for heaven's sake, watched her six employers with narrowed eyes. She didn't trust them, and she sure as heck didn't believe their cockamamie story about being brothers looking for the *simple* life.

The town—if one could call a tiny dot on the map surrounded by state parks and wildlife refuges and the Wind River Range of the Rockies, populated by only fifty people, many of them related, a *town*—had been abuzz since these six men had appeared six weeks ago. In the middle of winter. Ready to ranch.

Her ranch. Stolen out from under her by these…men. Who didn't *look or* act like any brothers she knew. Or ranchers, for that matter. They'd paid way over market price for the land and cattle—so much more than it was worth that her father simply hadn't been able to refuse their offer. And because of the outrageous amount, Dad had chosen to sell the ranch instead of passing the homestead down to her like he should have done.

But mostly Wildeans wanted to talk about the handsome, *single* out-of-towners, men who weren't related to any of their young daughters or nieces.

Zara didn't care about such frivolous, pointless nonsense. Zara wanted to know why they were *here.* And clearly lying. They weren't brothers in search of a simple life. For one, there was nothing simple about any of them. They were all tall and far too muscled. They all possessed a stillness and a wariness that made *her* nervous.

When she'd never been nervous a day in her life.

She'd helped them for over a month now, teaching them the ropes of how to run a ranch, even as they sank into the hard, uncompromising Wyoming winter— because they didn't know, of course. About ranching or real winters or *anything.*

Fortunately, they paid quite well for her tutoring, but a salary didn't earn trust.

Before they'd arrived, she'd called her cousin, a county deputy over in Bent, and he'd told her their backgrounds were clear.

Zara didn't believe it, but still, she taught them. Day in. Day out. Waiting for someone to slip up so she could figure out what their deal was.

They were quick learners. She'd give them that. They'd all taken to horseback riding easy as you please, except Dunne Thompson, who had some kind of injury which made getting up on the horse too difficult. They'd learned the lay of the land, the rhythms of ranch life. Quite frankly, Zara wasn't sure how much longer they'd keep her around—especially paying what they were paying.

But this was Hart land, and Zara was bound and determined to get it back once she figured out what these men were *really* up to.

Zara fingered the mane of the horse under her— they'd bought everything, down to Sam, her three-year-old mare. Her only saving grace was that she and Hazeleigh got to *rent* the dang cabin their great-grandpa had kicked the bucket in.

She looked at the men again. She understood men. Maybe she'd grown up in a house full of women, aside from Dad. Two sisters, identical because they were the Hart triplets. But she'd been the tomboy of the three girls. She liked ranching and sports and fighting.

These six weren't like the men she knew and had spent her life hanging out with. They were too…serious. Oh, they didn't all have the same personality. Six men were never *all* the same, but there was a guarded look in their eyes—which were all different shades and shapes—that matched.

Trauma could do that, she supposed. She figured hiding a body together or some such could too.

"All right, guys, you've got this side. I'm going to work from the other." She turned Sam around and ignored the offers to split up and help.

She didn't want their help or their proximity. They could work on fixing the fence from this side. She'd head several yards west and deal with the other broken section. Snow and ice wreaked havoc on a fence.

Zara eased Sam into a gallop and let the short ride clear her head. She was *almost* in a good mood when she pulled Sam to a stop. Until she saw Hazeleigh running toward her.

Zara sighed. She knew she should get down. Intercept Hazeleigh's wild run. Calm her sister down and tell her to take a breath.

Sometimes Zara felt like she was drowning under all the responsibilities left on her shoulders.

Hazeleigh came to a stop next to Sam, her hand immediately reaching out for purchase. She curled her fingers into Zara's pants leg.

"Stop. Don't."

"*Stop, don't* what?" Zara replied, resisting the urge to pull her leg away from Hazeleigh's grasp. "I was just going to fix the fence here."

Hazeleigh shook her head, dark hair whipping violently with the movement. "Don't."

Zara sighed at Hazeleigh's pale face, wide eyes and desperate pleas.

"Please, Haze, not another one of your 'feelings.'"

"Zee, really. Really. Something is wrong. You know I only say something when I can't get rid of it." She was grasping Zara's leg like it was a lifeline.

Zara hardly believed her sister could "feel" things. And sometimes her bad feelings came to nothing, so Zara felt confident in all that disbelief. Except when those bad feelings came to *something*, and someone—

usually Zara herself—narrowly missed out on being hurt or humiliated.

"What am I supposed to do? *Not* fix the fence and let the cattle get out?" Zara swung off Sam so she could be identical eye to identical eye with her sister. Except no one ever got them confused. They were too different, no matter how alike they looked.

Right now, Hazeleigh was wearing an oversize coat she'd forgotten to button and was next to threadbare anyway. Like most of what Hazeleigh wore, it was a thrift-store find. She wore pants—not jeans, not ranch wear—but some kind of vintage trousers that reminded Zara of the old movies Hazeleigh liked to watch. Her dark hair was a swirling mass around her, likely having fallen out of some colorful, silken scarf or old-fashioned pins, depending on if she was working or not today.

Zara, on the other hand, was in jeans, a flannel shirt and a cowboy hat. She never left home in anything other than her cowboy boots. She kept her long dark hair pulled back in a tight braid at all times.

"Just…" Hazeleigh looked at the place where the fence post was angled too far to the right. She reached out and grabbed Zara's hand. "You need to get away from here. We need to get away from here."

Zara pulled her hand away. Frustration warring with sympathy. Love warring with disdain. "I can't ignore my job."

"Everything okay?" came another voice, a deeper voice.

Zara glared at Jake Thompson's approach. She glared at all six of them all the time, whether they deserved it or not, but there was something about Jake that made her always want to glare extra hard.

He was too…watchful. Especially of *her*. She didn't care for it. At all. So she glared.

And he always smiled.

Hazeleigh shrunk away a little as he approached. Zara watched Jake notice it and react accordingly. He kept his distance.

Unfortunately, she had to give him credit for that.

As much as she *wanted* to believe they were killers who'd buried a body in a shallow grave and run away to hide from their misdeeds, they never made her afraid. Not just because she had guts, but because they were polite, careful and ever *aware*.

Of Hazeleigh's skittishness. Of not cornering either of them or standing too close. Of their own height and breadth and strength.

Zara wished they were a little less *honorable* just so she'd have better reason to dislike them.

"Everything is just fine," Zara said to Jake firmly.

"I was following to give you a hand, but then your sister came running like a bat out of hell. Usually that doesn't mean things are fine," Jake replied, a small smile on his face. She supposed it was his attempt at a *kind* smile.

Zara was not a fan of all the ways he tried to be nice when she was trying to dislike him.

"Maybe, but it's also very much none of your business."

"Zara," Hazeleigh murmured in admonition. She never could stand to see anyone act *rude*.

Which meant she was in a near-constant state of scolding Zara, who was quite often rude on purpose.

"Go home," Zara said to her sister, trying to keep her tone gentle. "I have work to do." She went over to the fence post and gave it a yank.

"Please don't," Hazeleigh whispered, but she stayed back. As if she was afraid of the very ground Zara was on.

"Go home, Hazeleigh," Zara said under her breath, but firm and a little harsh because she could not have this conversation in front of Jake. She got the fence post free in no time. The post had rotted away, and rot was never a good thing.

"I think we'll need to repour the foundation here," Zara said to Jake, ignoring her sister's stubborn presence. "Higher, so the wood doesn't have as much contact with the soil. It rotted too quickly. It's just not old enough to warrant this decay."

Jake nodded. "Something strange around here. Look at the snow. It almost looks like there's some kind of sinkhole underneath."

Zara frowned. Yes, that's exactly what it looked like. She tried to think the last time her father and she had worked in this area, but it was before any major snowfall. There shouldn't be this much difference in the landscape.

"Could be the wind," she offered, even though that didn't make sense either. Why would the wind blow snow away from this one spot?

Jake frowned at the ground, and Zara had to frown at it too. It was an odd place for a sinkhole. Not quite against the post or under the fence line but close enough to cause a problem.

"Maybe it's buried treasure." Jake grinned.

Zara had to fight very hard not to grin back. A ridiculous thought but kind of fun. "Maybe from that bank robbery back in 1892."

"You guys are really proud of that 130-year-old heist."

"The only thing interesting that's ever happened here," Zara said, trying to fight the feeling of easy camaraderie as they both grabbed short shovels from where Zara had packed them in the horse's saddle bag.

They wouldn't need to dig deep to get through the snow. The frozen ground might be an issue, but the other men could bring a post hole digger if necessary. Getting the fence back up was the most important thing.

They both began to clear the snow around where she'd removed the post. Once the snow was cleared, Jake dug in the hole left by the removed post. Zara knew she should too, but she couldn't stop looking at the strangely muddy ground next to where she stood. The grass hadn't grown back where the snow had accumulated less. Like someone had been digging just off the fence line.

She poked at it with her shovel, unable to ignore her curiosity. She didn't really think it was buried treasure, but it had to be something.

They needed to check before they poured more foundation here. Maybe something was causing the fence-post rot.

She jammed her shovel into the frozen patch. Not as frozen as it should be. She pulled out a chunk of dirt and then another. After a few scoops, her shovel hit something…strange. Not hard like an old cement foundation or anything of the like. Not frozen solid down below the surface. Hard but with an odd…soft give.

"Don't, don't, don't," Hazeleigh said desperately, covering her face with her hands. "Don't do it."

Zara looked at her sister. Dread curdled in her stomach, but how could she just ignore it? Maybe Hazeleigh's "feelings" had saved her from disaster once or twice, but what could be waiting in the earth that might harm her?

"Should we stop?" Jake asked, eyeing Hazeleigh balefully.

"No. She just… Ignore her. Here, I found something. Help me dig it out."

Jake nodded and moved closer to her. Too close. She could smell him. Soap and saddle leather. She could count the whiskers on his jawline that never seemed to fade no matter how often he shaved. She could see the glint of summer sky blue in his eyes. The sheer size of him, which oddly and unlike just about any other man she'd ever met, didn't make her want to challenge him.

And she did not care for her reaction to any of those things.

Jake let out a yelp of a curse, nearly falling backward as he scrambled away. She wanted to laugh at his reaction, tease him, but Hazeleigh's whispered *don't*s made her unable to come up with a smart remark.

"It's *you*," he said, looking at her like he'd seen a ghost.

Zara frowned, peering down into the hole Jake had made.

In an instant, her vision went gray. Because there was a face in the dirt.

One identical to hers.

JAKE MANAGED TO catch Zara before she tipped over like a tree that had just been felled. She was a sturdy woman, so it wasn't an easy catch.

Luckily he was strong enough to manage.

He looked back at the hole they'd dug. Had he really seen...?

Yeah, it was a face all right. Decaying a bit, but absolutely no doubt it looked exactly like the two women renting the cabin on the ranch. The two women standing right here.

"It's Amberleigh," Zara said. She sounded, for the first time in the six weeks he'd known her, rattled. She wasn't even standing on her own two feet. She was leaning on him as he held her upright.

A strange sensation, but one he didn't have time to analyze because there was a dead body buried on his property.

One who looked exactly like Zara and Hazeleigh.

"No," Hazeleigh was saying. Over and over again. "No, no."

Zara inhaled and exhaled noisily, then seemed to find her feet and took a step away from him. She wrapped her arms around herself as if that could hold her upright. "We need to... We have to..."

"Go on back to your cabin. I'll call the sheriff's department," Jake said. Though the dead body had surprised him, mostly because of how much it looked like their pretty ranch hand and her sister, it was hardly the first one he'd seen. Maybe he'd been optimistic enough to think he'd seen his last, but he'd get over his disappointment.

He didn't think these two women would be getting over this anytime soon.

"The police will want to talk to us," Zara said. She looked down at the ground like she wanted to look at the face again but couldn't bring herself to do it.

"Sure, but there's no reason you have to stand around here and wait." He put his hands on her shoulders. She stiffened but let him turn her away from the hole and toward her sister. Her *living* sister. "Go on."

Zara turned. Her chin came up, her eyes met his. "I'll stay with her."

Her. Meaning the dead body.

Hazeleigh reached out and grabbed Zara's hand. "We have to stay. And we should call Thomas… He'll handle it. Won't he?" Hazeleigh looked at Zara a little desperately.

Zara nodded faintly. Jake wasn't sure her eyes were really seeing anything. "Yes, I'll call Thomas," she said, her voice firm but tinny.

Shock. He'd seen a lot of that too. But Zara held firm as Hazeleigh began to cry quietly. Jake stood a few feet away, feeling at a loss.

Then instinct and habit kicked in. Maybe this was a ranch in the middle of nowhere, but he was a man who'd been trained to deal with too many disasters to name.

He sent a text to the guys explaining what had happened, warning them to stay back. As much as they could stay out of this, the better. He'd handle the police as much as possible.

Cops brought attention. Dead bodies brought *attention*. And that's what he and his "brothers" had come here to avoid.

But he couldn't rightly let Zara or her sister make the call, or stand here with another identical woman in the dirt. So, he called the sheriff's department himself. He spoke with a dispatcher, gave his details too many times to count, asked for the mysterious Thomas the sisters seemed to want and then settled in to wait.

It took too long. Hazeleigh was a mess by the time a lone cop got out of a marked car over by the main house. Zara stood firm, holding on to her sister, but it was the kind of firm that was just seconds away from breaking.

Jake watched the cop's approach. He was a middle-aged gentleman. Late forties maybe, tall with just the hint of a paunch. He wore a brown uniform and didn't seem to be any hurry.

Jake tried to keep the scowl off his face. He didn't like cops on a good day. He knew it wasn't a *fair* feeling, but knowing and feeling were two separate things. But he immediately didn't like *this* cop and his lack of hurry.

"Zara. Hazeleigh," the deputy said, nodding at each of the women. He turned to Jake, suspicion in his eyes. "And you're one of the ranch owners?" he said with some distaste.

Mostly the town of Wilde had been friendly. But

there were a few who weren't happy that Lee Hart had sold. And a few, mostly men, who put the blame for that unhappiness on the buyers' shoulders. Not the seller's.

"Jake Thompson." Jake had to beat back his desire to sneer at the man. He held out a hand instead and forced his mouth to curve. "Good to meet you. Wish it was under better circumstances."

The deputy nodded. "So, what's the problem?"

That was the thing about cops. They asked questions they knew the answers to. Hadn't he gotten a dispatch call? Didn't he *know* the problem?

Jake pointed at the hole, at just about the same time Zara did. Seemed neither of them felt like answering the question.

The cop stepped forward, peered into the hole, then stumbled back. "Holy hell," the cop said, his voice breaking. "It's…"

"Amberleigh," Zara finished for him. "Yes, Steven. Now, can we please get her out of the ground? Find out what…?" Zara's voice cracked, but she ruthlessly cleared her throat.

Jake had seen a lot of people do hard things in terrible circumstances. He'd seen acts of bravery and courage, failure and weakness. But Zara clearing her throat and saying the rest as she held on to Hazeleigh's shaking frame struck him as particularly poignant.

"We need to know what happened," she said firmly, her eyes on *Steven* the cop. "Where's Thomas?"

"This isn't his sector, Zara. Hell. Just… Okay." He took a deep breath, clearly rattled. "I didn't expect…"

"Steven," Zara said, her voice sharp. "Get it together."

The cop nodded and swallowed. He pulled his radio off his chest and began to mutter into it. Jake crossed to Zara and Hazeleigh. "Go home. I'll handle this."

"We should be here with her," Zara said, looking at the hole in the ground. They couldn't see the face from here, but Jake knew from experience Zara would see it in her mind's eye, probably forever.

Jake blew out a breath and put his hand on Zara's shoulder. A strong shoulder, but this was too much for anyone. "You can't do anything for her now except take care of yourselves." He nodded toward Hazeleigh.

Zara looked at her sister. A pale, shaking mess. She exhaled and nodded, care for her sister overriding the need to stay here and be strong.

"Come on, Haze," she said. "We should go home. We can't do anything here."

"I knew it was bad, Zara. I knew it was bad."

"I know. You were right," Zara said, turning Hazeleigh around, and they began to walk toward their cabin, horse forgotten. That was fine. Jake would take care of it.

He probably shouldn't. His job here, all six of their jobs here was to lay low. Avoid attention. Blend in.

A dead body on their property wasn't going to do that. Especially if he *handled* things for Zara and Hazeleigh.

"Jake?" Zara said, looking over her shoulder.

"Yeah?"

She gave him a firm nod. "Thanks," she said and then looked away, walking with Hazeleigh toward their cabin.

Yeah, he'd find a way to take care of it. That's all there was to it.

Chapter Two

Zara's head pounded after the phone call to her father. He'd refused to believe her, and she could hardly blame him for that. The police would verify the body tomorrow, and maybe that would convince him. Or maybe time would sink the truth into him. He needed time.

Zara didn't. Zara knew her own dead face looking up at her meant Amberleigh was dead, and there was no getting away from that.

But the part she couldn't work out, the part that didn't make sense, was Amberleigh being buried *here*. And if she looked just like Zara's reflection in the mirror and Hazeleigh's face when she wasn't drawn and pale, it meant she hadn't died when she'd run away at sixteen.

She'd died recently. And *here*.

It was something that sat in Zara's mind like an immovable stone. She ate supper with Hazeleigh in mutual silence, and then, when no one from the sheriff's department called or came by, they went to bed.

Zara didn't sleep and, based on the dark circles under Hazeleigh's eyes the next morning, she didn't think her sister had either.

"I've got to go check on the guys and make sure they did the chores," Zara said, feeling a mix of guilt and relief she had something to do. Somewhere to go. The cabin was too stuffy. Hazeleigh's grief was too…

Hazeleigh nodded vaguely. She had a mug in front of her but had never poured anything into it. Still she stared like it had all the answers. The little Christmas tree Hazeleigh had put in the middle of the kitchen table when she'd decorated for Christmas the day after Thanksgiving felt cheerful and so damn out of place.

"Haze…"

Hazeleigh shook her head, eyes filling with tears. "Why didn't I have a feeling before she was dead?"

Zara reached over and took Hazeleigh's hand. "It's not your fault. Honey, you put way too much stock in those feelings. Maybe you've got a sixth sense or something, but you can't save people from *murderers*. Amberleigh… She had to have been mixed-up in something."

"I saved you from that car accident."

"It was luck, Hazeleigh. Luck." Or a coincidence that Hazeleigh's desperate phone call a few years back had prompted her to pull off the road, and then yes, not be crushed by debris that had fallen onto the road in front of her seconds later. Luck, coincidence or some weird paranormal feeling, it didn't matter. She couldn't let Hazeleigh feel responsible for this.

Zara searched for the words. Comforting ones weren't easy for her, but this was so unfair. Hazeleigh couldn't control her flights of fancy, regardless of what they were, and Dad had… Dad had really done a number on her when Amberleigh had disappeared. Insisting Hazeleigh should be able to figure out where she'd gone, with her "feelings."

Just because life had been *boring* in Wilde didn't mean it wasn't without complications. Especially the family-ties kind.

"Maybe I should be the one to call Dad," Hazeleigh said, looking at her hands. "He hates me anyway."

"Dad doesn't hate you. He's a mean old jackass who doesn't know how to process his feelings, but he doesn't *hate* you. Besides, I already called him. He didn't believe me."

Hazeleigh shook her head sadly. "He hates me. And Amberleigh's dead, so that's not going to change." By the time she got to the end of the sentence, her voice was just a squeak. "How can she be dead?"

"The cops will figure it out. They have to." Zara thought of Thomas. He was a good cop, but related to them, so he wouldn't be able to work on the case. Still, he'd be able to make sure it didn't fall through the cracks. "You know, the guys are doing pretty good on their own. I can skip chores and—"

"Don't. I know I seem fragile, and maybe I am a bit, but...I don't need to be sheltered from it." She clutched her hands into fists on the table in front of her. "I don't need a mother hen."

Zara wasn't so sure about that, but she was hardly going to argue over it. Maybe Hazeleigh needed some alone time. Zara would give it to her. For a half hour anyway. She'd just go find the guys and tell them she was taking the day off.

Normally it would kill her to ask for a day off, but she figured uncovering your dead identical-triplet's body buried on your family ranch was grounds for a day off.

She'd rather work through this strange mix of old grief—because truth be told, she'd already assumed her sister was dead or she would have come slinking back long ago—and guilt, because she *had* thought that and hadn't done anything about it.

Even knowing no one had ever been able to do a thing about Amberleigh. People thought *Zara* was stubborn, but she hadn't held a candle to her sister.

Who was dead.

Dead.

Zara closed her eyes against the heavy weight of it. It felt more real than it had when she'd simply believed it was true. More horrifying when she'd seen the evidence. She blew out a breath, gathering all her strength.

She wouldn't be emotional when she talked to the Thompson brothers. She'd be matter-of-fact. That's what this situation needed. Practicality. Sturdiness.

Hallmarks of who she was.

"Call if you need me," Zara said to Hazeleigh, shrugging on her coat and shoving her feet into her boots by the front door. She opened the door to find Thomas standing there, hand raised like he'd been about to knock. He was wearing his Bent County Sheriff's Department uniform.

That was not a good sign.

"Zara."

"Thomas. You…" She looked beyond him to a blonde woman standing there. She wasn't in a uniform, but that somehow made it worse.

"Zara, this is Detective Laurel Delaney-Carson. We've got a few questions for Hazeleigh."

Zara was about to step out of the doorway and let them in, but then what he said fully registered. She didn't move. "Why Hazeleigh?"

Thomas looked back at the detective. He didn't answer her question. "This is Zaraleigh. The other sister."

The woman smiled kindly, a mix of briskness and empathy that made Zara less inclined to hate her on sight.

"We're sorry to bother you so early, Zara. But the sooner we get started, the sooner we can find out what happened to Amberleigh."

"Why do you only want to talk to Hazeleigh? *I'm* the one who found her."

The detective pulled a notebook out of her coat pocket. "You and your employer, Jake Thompson?"

"Did I hear my name?"

Everyone on the porch slowly turned. And there he was. Striding up the yard, looking as he always did. Jeans, cowboy boots that were finally starting to look worn-in rather than brand-new. A cowboy hat that she hated to admit looked just right on him.

But this wasn't right. At all. "What are you doing here?"

"Just thought I'd bring by some breakfast," Jake said, smiling genially. As if he often…came into their cabin offering pastries, when he, in fact, *never* did. All the Thompsons gave their cabin a very wide berth.

But he was holding a white bakery bag, like he had brought breakfast. She studied his face skeptically, but his expression was all cheerful friendliness.

She didn't trust it for a minute.

"Mr. Thompson," the detective said. "I'm Detective Delaney-Carson." She held out her hand for a professional handshake. "I'm working the case about the dead body found on your property. I'll have some questions for you, but I'd like to talk to Hazeleigh Hart first. Perhaps you and Zara could wait out here with Deputy H—"

"No," Zara said, realizing with a start Jake had said the same thing in unison. She stared up at him, her eyebrows drawing together. What game was this guy playing?

JAKE WAS NO stranger to irritated females glaring at him. He'd had foster sisters once upon a time. They hadn't cared for him. He'd never been able to blame them for it, any more than he could blame Zara or the detective.

"It's procedure," Detective What's-her-names said. Firmly.

Zara opened her mouth, but Jake talked over her. Smoothly. Charmingly, if he did say so himself. "I'm sure it is, but Hazeleigh's pretty beat-up about this. Isn't she, Zara?"

"Of course. Understandably," Zara said, as if she was defending Hazeleigh to *him*. When he was trying to help.

Damn prickly woman.

"Understandably," Jake agreed gently. "She needs some support. Surely you can ask Hazeleigh your questions with Zara there to support her sister."

"I'm afraid I can't. I'll need to interview you all separately. It's absolutely necessary. I brought Thomas, though, because he's family. He can't be an active investigator on the case, but I thought a friendly face would help both of you feel more comfortable answering questions," the detective said pointedly to Zara and leaving him out of the equation.

Zara's gaze turned to this Thomas. A family member. Jake studied the tall, fair deputy. Not much of a family resemblance.

"We don't want to make this harder on any of you than it needs to be," the detective continued. "But we need to conduct an airtight investigation. So, if you two can promise to stay here, I'll take Thomas in and talk to Hazeleigh, so she'll have support."

She looked at Jake and then Zara, as if waiting for their agreement. He'd give her some credit for giving the illusion that they had any say in the matter.

Zara looked at the cop—her cousin, apparently. "I'm holding you to that, Thomas."

The cop looked a little hurt by Zara's guilt trip. "Come on, Zara. You know me."

Her frown turned into something else. Guilt or grief with a heavy dose of frustration. "Fine," she muttered.

She pushed past the cop and the detective and then him and marched her way through the front yard to a big tree that had a cracked, uneven concrete bench underneath.

Jake met the cop and detective's shrewd gazes but, in the end, decided not to say anything. He turned and followed Zara to the bench, the sound of the cops entering the cabin echoing in the quiet morning around them.

Jake stood in front of Zara. She sat, hands clenched around the edge of the bench, looking at her boots.

"Why are you here?" she asked, with just enough bitterness to make the lost look on her face less terrifying.

"We figured you'd want the day off, and your stubborn head wouldn't think to take it. I lost the coin toss to come tell you." The second half was a lie, but it suited his purposes. Keep his brothers out of it as much as he could.

She snorted. From his vantage point of looking at her bowed profile, she looked pissed and pale and exhausted but not exactly…wrecked. Like he'd maybe expected under the circumstances.

She turned that sharp brown gaze on him. "If you're looking for signs of a frantic female, you won't find it."

"I wasn't looking. I just… Your sister is dead."

Zara shrugged. "I've thought she was dead for years. It's awful to have it confirmed, but it's not exactly a shock. I didn't need…that kind of proof." She shuddered.

And didn't tell him to go away so he slid onto the bench next to her. Giving her as much space as he could on the small slab of concrete. "What's her story?"

"She ran away. When we were sixteen. Haven't heard from her since. She was…" Zara trailed off, something like a wince crossing her features. "It feels wrong to speak ill of the dead."

"Consider it giving me and my brothers the pertinent information to understand what's going on when we're inevitably all questioned."

She frowned at him. "Why would they question all of you? You were the only one with me."

"It's our land." And there'd be speculation. Investigation. When they could little afford this kind of attention.

"Ah," she said, shaking her head and giving a little laugh. "*That's* why you're here. You're worried you're going to be a suspect." She seemed to mull that over, looking at him skeptically. Then she let out a disgusted breath. "I want to think it's you. That'd be easy. But you could have kept us away from that spot. Beyond that, I saw how damn surprised you were. You thought it was me. You didn't know there was a third. Unless you're a really good actor. But that's not my place to decide. I'll tell the detective you thought it was me. You'll be in the clear because I know it wasn't you." She frowned at the cabin. "Why Hazeleigh first? *I* uncovered the body."

Like Zara, he looked back at the cabin. It was a valid question, and a concerning one. "She warned you. She didn't want you to dig there."

She shook her head. "They wouldn't know that. You were the only one who—" She jumped up, outraged. "You *told* them that."

He held up his hands and stayed seated so as not to give the impression he was fighting with her. "Zara, I answered the questions they asked when I made the call."

"You told them. You… This is all your fault. Go home, Jake. To *my* home that you stole from me, and stay the hell away from me and my family." She marched for the cabin, and no doubt she'd be in trouble for bursting in.

And no doubt he'd just screwed up his chance to

make this less dramatic. To keep the attention far away from him and his brothers.

Who were really, *really* not going to be happy about the new developments.

Chapter Three

Zara stopped herself in the entry to the cabin. If she barged into the kitchen where she could hear the low tones of talking, it would complicate…everything.

But they couldn't honestly be in there with the thought *Hazeleigh* had something to do with it. She stood there, torn by indecision, breathing a little too heavily. She needed to get her temper, her anger under control before she went in there.

But that was hard for her on a good day.

After a long while, Thomas left the kitchen and saw her standing at the doorway. He smiled kindly. "Do you have time for some questions?"

She nodded.

"Hazeleigh went out back, into the garden. She said she was looking for the cat, but I think she needed some air. Some alone time."

Zara managed a nod. "Look, I can handle this questioning thing on my own. Will you stay with her?"

Thomas nodded, but he reached out and gave her shoulder a little squeeze. "She's not as fragile as you seem to think. She held up pretty well."

But "pretty well" wasn't good enough, was it? Zara

stepped away from Thomas's hand and stepped into her own kitchen, feeling like a stranger. The detective had a small array of things spread out before her on the table in a neat, nearly anal fashion. Notebook, phone, two pens. All at the same angle.

The Christmas tree had been moved to the kitchen counter, and Hazeleigh's Christmas-themed mug sat in the sink as if she'd actually used it this morning.

The detective looked up at Zara and offered a kind smile. "Have a seat, Ms. Hart."

"Call me Zara," Zara muttered. It felt so formal to be called *Ms*.

"Do you want anything before we start?"

Zara shook her head. She just wanted this over with. She told herself not to be petty. They all wanted to get to the bottom of this. And the only way to do that was with clear, concise, *honest* answers.

But, oh, how she wished she could throw Jake Thompson under the bus.

The detective took a breath. "Before we start, I just want you to know, it's my job to find out the truth—regardless of what that truth is. I assume we're after the same thing, but I also know what it's like to have a sister you want to protect."

"Hazeleigh didn't kill our sister," Zara said firmly. It was the *truth*. The only truth.

"Why do you think you need to say that?" the detective asked, void of any inflection or any implication, but Zara felt them all the same.

"You interviewed her first when I was the one who uncovered the body. Well, Jake and I." She'd throw him a *little* under the bus. If only with the truth.

"I'm just here to ask questions."

Zara muttered an oath, then closed her eyes. "Sorry," she offered to the detective.

"No need to apologize. I've heard worse. Look, Zara, this is a trauma that you're going through, and it's going to have emotional responses. Especially this time of year. Emotions don't follow the rules. I'm not here to judge your emotions, *or* your sister's. I'm here to get to the bottom of the crime *and* to make sure we've built an airtight case when we do find out who did this. It's why Thomas can't be a bigger part of the investigation. It risks our credibility down the line. I won't risk anything on this case, I promise you that."

Zara frowned at the detective. She had to give the woman credit—she knew what to say to help… Zara couldn't say she felt better, but it eased some of those high-strung nerves. "Have you worked a lot of murders?"

"A lot? No. It is Bent County after all." She smiled kindly. "But this isn't my first murder case, no. So believe me when I say I need your cooperation and your honesty so we can make sure we get the person who did this and see them punished."

Zara nodded and swallowed. "Okay. How can I help?"

The detective tapped her phone. The home picture was of a smiling family. A Carson-Delaney family. Because she was one of the ones Bent had made such a stink about a few years back, because the Carsons and Delaneys were supposed to hate each other. A modern-day Hatfield and McCoy situation.

Apparently, now the enemies had two cute kids.

The detective swiped the picture away and brought up a recorder of some kind. "I'm going to take notes and record the conversation." She noted the date and time and Zara's full name, to Zara's distaste, and then looked up at Zara. Her gaze was frank but not unkind. "Let's start with how you found the body."

Zara went through the whole thing. She was honest, even when it came to Hazeleigh. The detective really made her feel like…well, like if she told the truth everything would be okay. The whole truth.

"She has these feelings," Zara said, unable to stop herself from wincing at the word. "She always has." Zara looked up at the detective imploringly. "She once saved me from a car accident. I know that sounds crazy, but she *does* get these feelings sometimes. Hazeleigh wouldn't hurt a fly. She wouldn't know *how*."

The detective smiled, and it was kind but…guarded. "It's good to have that kind of impression of your sister. And, I hope you understand that I'm not trying to be dismissive when I say feelings aren't evidence."

Zara sighed. No, she couldn't blame the detective for that.

"That's all I need from you and Hazeleigh today. Likely we'll have follow-up questions, either in person or by phone. We'll continue to interview those involved. Jake Thompson. The first officer on the scene. We'll wait for the coroner's report to give us an idea of when she died and other details that will help us come up with a timeline and some suspects." The detective began to pack up her items in a small bag. When she was finished, she held out a hand to Zara.

Zara shook it, a heavy weight in her stomach, but the detective held on. Gave her hand a squeeze.

"I will do everything in my power to find your sister's killer."

Zara managed a smile. "Thank you."

The detective dropped her hand, looked at the door in the kitchen, presumably the one Hazeleigh went out of. "Thomas was right when he told you she held up well." Her eyes returned to Zara's, frank and assessing. "But she's hiding something. I'd encourage her to tell me. Sooner rather than later."

Zara could only frown at the detective's retreating back.

Hazeleigh wasn't hiding anything. They didn't have secrets.

But that heavy weight didn't move, and for the first time in a very long time, Zara didn't know where to turn.

"You understand that this is a disaster, right?"

Jake lounged on the couch in the living room of the creaky old ranch house that was almost starting to feel like home. Not that Jake was well versed in what *homes* felt like, but if he thought back to his childhood dreaming of what one might be like, it would be a lot like this.

Spacious. Old. Newer little additions added on over the years in weird angles and uneven transitions between rooms.

It wasn't perfect or shiny or boring. So, yeah, he'd grown fond of the place.

But that didn't mean he'd found anything *easy* about the transition. Especially when Cal stood before him, legs spread, hands clasped behind his back, disapproving frown on his face.

Like they were back in training.

A dichotomy to that *homey* feel.

"Jake," Cal barked.

Jake sighed. Six weeks into their supposed new lives and Cal still acted like the commanding officer he wasn't supposed to be anymore.

"I didn't kill her and bury her on our property, so I don't see why you're lecturing me about it," Jake replied. He forced himself to remain relaxed, because they *weren't* in the military together anymore and he did not have to stand at attention to Cal or anyone else.

Truth be told, Jake was warming up to civilian life pretty quick. Cal…not so much.

"I guess you don't recall our mission when we were assigned here."

Jake shook his head, careful to keep his voice even instead of frustrated, because Cal thrived on frustration and dissent—in that, he thrived on stamping it out. It made him a hell of a commander.

Not such a great characteristic for a "brother."

"We're not on a *mission*, Cal. We're not on *assignment*. We've been hidden away. Stripped of all our ranks, responsibilities and connections. This is just supposed to be…life."

Cal's mouth firmed. He didn't like that reminder. That he wasn't in charge. That he didn't have a goal to accomplish other than fly under the radar.

Cal wasn't ready for all this *non*military life.

Jake might have felt sorry for him if he wasn't so worried. "Did you tell the boss?" he asked, infusing his voice and body with a casualness that was very much an act.

The boss. Major General Wilks, though they usually just referred to him as *the boss*, was their one and only connection to the old life. The life they'd had to leave because they were all marked men. Doomed to die if they didn't disappear.

So they'd come to the most out-of-the-way, boring place the boss could secure.

And somehow they'd stumbled upon a dead body. Not exactly the quiet life they were looking for.

Would the military make them move again? Erase these identities too? Start all over. *Again*. The idea made Jake…uncomfortable. At best.

"No, I haven't told him. Ideally, this all gets figured out in a few days and he's none the wiser, or doesn't know until the case is put to bed and we're squarely out of the spotlight." Cal didn't rake his hands through his hair or pace his frustration away. He stood there, military straight, completely immobile.

But Jake had been with Cal long enough to know that he *wanted* to do all those things. Would he ever let go and actually…let himself be normal again? With a little pang, Jake kind of doubted it.

"Look, maybe the cops ask a few questions, but whoever buried that body…" Jake suppressed a shudder at Zara's face in the dirt, unseeing and lifeless.

Amberleigh Hart. Not Zara. Hard to remember, even when there were two replicas of that same face walking around, that it wasn't Zara's body they'd found in the ground.

"Whoever did all this did it before we owned the

land. They're not going to be looking at us too hard. It just doesn't make sen—"

His words were cut off by a firm, no-nonsense knock on the door. A *cop* knock. Cal gave Jake an eyebrows-raised look. One that clearly said "told you so."

Cal walked to the front door and opened it to the blonde detective. She studied Cal, sized him up quickly. Her smile was polite if distant. "Hello, I need to speak with Jake Thompson."

"And you are?"

"Detective Delaney-Carson. I just have a few questions for Mr. Thompson. To be asked of him. Alone," she said pointedly.

"Is he a suspect?" Cal demanded, point-blank.

The woman didn't flinch or bat an eye. She met Cal's glare with a bland one. "Everyone's a suspect right now. And you are?"

Cal's face went carefully blank, and no matter how smart this detective was, Jake was pretty sure he was the only one in the room who knew how much energy Cal was putting into that blankness.

"Cal Thompson."

The detective nodded. "One of the brothers." She turned her attention to Jake, behind Cal. "Is there somewhere we can speak alone?"

Jake nodded in assent, and with obvious reluctance, Cal stepped aside and let her enter. Jake jerked his chin toward the kitchen. "Follow me."

He led her into the small old kitchen and gestured for her to take a seat at the table Jake thought might be from the 1800s, it was so old and scarred. "Can I get you anything to drink?"

"No, this should be quick enough." She set her bag down on the kitchen table, pulled out a phone and a notebook. "No Christmas decorations?" she asked casually as she took a seat in a kitchen.

"Still in storage," Jake returned with the easy lie.

She didn't react. "I just need you to run through what you saw and did yesterday."

"To see if my story matches everyone else's?" he asked, standing.

She looked up at him with sharp brown eyes. She might be a little thing, but she wasn't a pushover. "To do my job, Mr. Thompson."

Jake sighed. "Call me Jake," he muttered. "I already ran through this when I called in what we found."

She nodded. "You did. Let's run through it again." She clicked a button on her phone, noted the date and time, and then asked him questions. She didn't ask him to sit. She didn't fill in any blanks. She just asked question after question.

And she didn't lie. It was quick. After he went through the ten minutes or so he'd been involved, the detective turned off the recording, closed her notebook and then studied him. Carefully. "Zara said that Hazeleigh gets these…feelings. Like premonitions," she said at very long length.

When the detective didn't ask a question after that statement, Jake shrugged. "Okay."

"You haven't had any experience with these…feelings?"

"Hazeleigh lives in that cabin with her sister, and that's the extent of what I know about her. I work with Zara on the day-to-day, but that doesn't exactly make us close. We've only been here six weeks. And you likely know Zara enough to know she didn't relish her father selling the ranch to us."

She nodded, then smiled and got to her feet. "Thank you for your time, Mr. Thompson."

"I'll walk you out," he said, feeling oddly…unsettled. Like that hadn't gone the way it should have. The feeling only intensified when they walked into the living room and Cal was still standing there, arms crossed.

The detective followed Jake to the door, pausing her exit as Jake held it open.

"It'd help a lot if you stay put for the time being. No trips or leaving the county without letting us know." She shrugged. "As a precaution." She turned to survey Cal. "That goes for all six of you, actually." Then she left.

The silence she left behind was…*heavy*.

A dull pounding started at the base of Jake's skull. He wasn't a suspect. Not seriously. *They* weren't, but they weren't exactly out of the woods and…they couldn't afford that kind of scrutiny.

"We're screwed," Cal said flatly. "I'm calling the boss."

"No. We're not." Jake looked at Cal. It was hard on a good day to talk Cal out of something, but this… He didn't want to be uprooted again. They'd worked this ranch for a month and Jake had let himself get…settled.

He wouldn't leave. Not on the damn boss's whim. For once *he* was going to have a say on where he went, where he *stayed*. He was too damn old to keep having someone else yank the strings of his life. "You like it here, don't you?"

Cal shook his head grimly. "It's not our call."

Which was as close to a yes as Cal was ever going to get. "But it could be our call." Jake wanted to reach out and shake Cal, but he kept his hands at his sides. "All we have to do is figure out who did this so it's all over before the boss gets wind."

"You're not a cop," Cal said, but there was just enough give in his voice Jake figured he was getting somewhere.

Jake grinned. "No, even better. I'm a soldier."

Chapter Four

When two uniformed cops returned to their cabin the next morning with a *search warrant*, Zara knew things were bad.

When they left the house with some of Hazeleigh's personal items, she knew things were catastrophic.

Hazeleigh's silent, unemotional accepting of it all was…beyond disconcerting. It scared Zara down to her bones. Hazeleigh was *always* emotional. About everything—kittens, Hallmark movies, the perfect piece of fudge.

But not the fact police had *seized* her belongings.

"I think I'll go in to work," Hazeleigh said, still sitting at the kitchen table staring at the door the cops had gone out of not fifteen minutes before. Christmas lights twinkled around the frame. "I'm falling behind and Mr. Field thinks he's *this* close to a breakthrough."

Hazeleigh worked as a research assistant for an eccentric old man who was determined to find out what had happened to the alleged gold stolen from the bank robbery back in 1892. A fool's errand, in Zara's estimation, but Hazeleigh liked losing herself in old newspapers and mysteries, and the crazy old man paid well.

"Mr. Field always thinks he's *this* close to a break-through," Zara replied.

Hazeleigh smiled faintly.

Zara wanted to shake her, but she was afraid Hazeleigh would break apart. Dissolve. Or wind up buried in the ground just like Amberleigh.

"Is there something you're not telling me?" Zara asked, holding on so tight to the counter behind her she would no doubt have a hand cramp.

Hazeleigh's eyes widened. It might have been funny, the attempt at innocence, if innocence weren't absolutely imperative here.

"Haze."

Hazeleigh smiled. "Don't worry so much, Zara. Everything is fine. I hardly killed Amberleigh."

"I hardly think you did. But I don't like the thought that you're keeping things from me. That you're not taking this seriously."

Hazeleigh opened her mouth to respond, but the creak of a door and their father's gravelly voice calling out a greeting had them both flinching.

Hazeleigh jumped to her feet. "I'll just leave out the back."

"Hazeleigh."

She shook her head, grabbing her bag from where it hung off the back of her chair. "He won't want to see me, or if he does, it's only to be mean."

Zara couldn't argue with that, so she let Hazeleigh scurry out the back door. She huffed out a breath and held herself very still as her father entered the kitchen.

She forced a small, fake smile. "Dad, what are you doing here so early?"

He looked around the kitchen. The years had dug the lines into his face, the cigarettes he refused to give up had hewed his body down to a shade too skinny. Or maybe that was all the grief he held at arm's length. Or was it the alcoholism they all refused to acknowledge?

"Just you?" he asked.

"Hazeleigh went to work, which is where I need to be headed." But she didn't make a move to leave.

"I don't know how you live here with her. After yesterday, how you'd share a roof with her."

"Dad—"

"She could have found her all this time, and now Amberleigh is dead."

"She couldn't find her," Zara said firmly. Maybe Hazeleigh was uncharacteristically keeping something from her, but she hadn't been able to reach Amberleigh. Even if she could have reached their sister, what were the chances Amberleigh would have come home?

"I don't believe that."

"*I* do." Zara pinched the bridge of her nose. She'd always had to be the responsible one. Dad and Amberleigh fighting. Dad being too hard on Hazeleigh. And always Zara herself stepping in and getting things *accomplished*.

But she didn't know how to accomplish this, and it scared her more than anything. "We need to make arrangements." She wouldn't argue with him about Hazeleigh. It wasn't worth it. They had to focus on practicalities. "The detective said they won't be able to release the body for a few days yet, but we need to make arrangements."

"My daughter is dead."

My sister is dead. But she didn't say it. "Do you want me to handle things?"

He gave a curt nod. "All these people calling me. I don't want it. I can't even walk through town without someone saying something to me."

They're called condolences. It's called care. The town wants to grieve with you.

They'd walked down this road before. When Mom had died. Even then, Zara had spared his feelings. Taken on the responsibilities.

She'd been eight.

"I'll take care of it." It was what she could do, so she'd do it.

He looked around the cabin. "Don't know how you can live here. Work here."

"What other choice did I have?" Dad hadn't exactly offered to split the money he got for the sale.

"Keep the old ladies off my doorstep, huh?"

I love you too. This hurts too much. I don't know what to do. But she said nothing. After all, she'd had eighteen years to learn sentimentality wouldn't get her anywhere. "Dad?"

He looked back, and honestly, nothing had changed. Dad had been this way since Mom died, and Zara had stepped up to take up the slack. Why would Amberleigh's murder be any different?

But what she wouldn't do for a hug and a promise things would be okay.

"If you can't be nice to Hazeleigh, there's no point in you coming all the way out. Just call me if you need something."

He nodded. Unhurt. *People have to care about*

something besides themselves to be hurt. "All right." He nodded and walked out. No goodbye. No comforting words. Just what he needed Zara to do.

So, she'd do it. All it would take was one call to Mrs. Vickers. She'd explain that Dad preferred their offers of grief to come through her. Mrs. Vickers would spread it around—the quilting club, the convenience store, the bank. Everyone would know.

And they wouldn't bring casseroles. They wouldn't ask if she needed any help. Zara Hart didn't need those things.

But she'd give Wildeans credit for one thing. They'd give her something her father hadn't.

A kind word. Maybe a hug.

As for everything else? Zara would take care of it the way she always did.

WHEN JAKE FINALLY found Zara that morning, she was in the horse stable, saddling up her horse like she was just…going to work today.

"I hope you know you don't have to do that."

She didn't look back at him as she fastened the saddle into place. "Do what? Saddle my horse? Kind of a requirement for riding her."

He didn't miss the way she said *my.* A not-so-subtle reminder she belonged here. And maybe a little dig that he didn't.

But he'd let it go because God know she was hurting. "Still mad at me?"

She let out a gusty sigh, and for a second, her shoulders slumped as if the weight of anger was just too much to bear. Then she straightened her shoulders and shook her head, staring at the horse's flank. "I couldn't lie to the detective. How can I expect you to?"

Which wasn't a no, exactly, but he'd take it.

Zara pushed past him and pulled her horse outside. Jake followed along, trying to work out how he was going to approach this. He needed to know what Zara and Hazeleigh had talked to the cops about, where the detective was leaning. He could approach Hazeleigh, but she could be skittish.

Zara seemed infinitely capable of…everything. Questions, certainly. But would the prickly woman offer him any information? Well, all he could do was try. "Landon said the cops were here. Early." He said it casually. As if he wasn't fishing for information.

Zara nodded in confirmation. "You gonna work today or just repeat what everyone already knows?"

He'd planned on focusing on the case rather than ranch work—there were five other people to take up the slack, but Zara was part of the case, wasn't she? "Sure, just let me get *my* horse."

She muttered something that sounded suspiciously like "your horse my ass." But she waited, and when he led his own horse outside, she was sitting in the saddle. Her gaze was on the jagged mountains in the far distance, an odd yearning on her face that had something tightening in his gut.

He wasn't *blind*. He'd noticed she was attractive before. And she was different from her sister. Hazeleigh was pretty but skittish. Fragile.

Zara was strong and unafraid and… He studied her profile for a second as he settled himself in the saddle.

Today? None of her usual…vitality. She looked tired.

Weighed down by the truly horrible situation she found herself in.

"You really don't have to work today," Jake said, trying to find some balance between gentle, which would put her back up, and dismissive, which might hurt her feelings. Not that she'd ever show it. "This is the kind of thing people take personal time for. Grievance time. You'd still be paid."

She squinted out over the rolling hills, the endless white of a snow-covered landscape, the blue sky, the puffy white clouds. All the way to those imposing mountains that had stood the test of time in a way Jake, who'd been born and bred in Pittsburgh, wasn't sure he'd ever understand. Or not be in awe of.

It was a bucolic picture. But more than that for her, no doubt. A home and legacy. Which were things he didn't know anything about—except that as a foster kid who'd never belonged anywhere but in the military, he envied that she had anything like it.

"This is my grievance time," she said, and the delivery was unemotional and quiet, but it landed with the effect of a sob. Something sharp and jagged twisted in his chest.

When she nudged her horse into a trot, he followed, saying nothing. But he was using the skills *she'd* taught him to ride the horse, and it felt like…something.

He'd never even had a dog. Animals were as foreign to him as *home*, but he liked the strange partnership between beast and man. The way the horse was a tool, but also a living, breathing thing, and they had to work together to get from one place to another.

He followed her, trusting where she'd lead and the

speed she set their horses on. They rode for a while, the cold wind whipping at their faces. It wasn't a half-bad way to spend a morning, all in all. Something that shocked Jake just about every day he woke up here happy to start the day.

When she pulled her horse to a stop on the slope of a hill with a strange rock tower at the top rising out of the snow, Jake was no closer to knowing what they were doing. And when she just sat on her horse looking out at the land around them, he wondered if even she knew.

It was early enough that the moon was still a white ball, incongruous to the day sky. Zara stared at it like it might hand her an answer or two.

Jake didn't know how long they sat there. He'd waited in enough silences to know not to count the seconds. To simply find something to focus on, think about. To keep his eyes and ears open and wait without expectation.

A strand of hair had escaped her braid and danced in the wind and that was what he focused on while he waited.

Eventually, she blew out a breath, that stoic gaze faltering for a second. "They seized some of Hazeleigh's things."

He frowned over that information. "They have a warrant?"

She nodded. No matter how hard she worked to look unaffected, worry was in the set of her eyebrows. The purse of her lips.

Jake felt like he had to ask. "Is it possible…?"

Zara stiffened, scowled at him as she adjusted her grip on her reins. "Not even remotely."

Jake nodded, holding her accusing stare. "Who would want to hurt your sister? Either sister?"

She blinked. Then frowned down at her hands. "The detective asked me that, but Amberleigh wasn't here. I haven't seen or heard from her since we were sixteen. So how would I know on that score? And Hazeleigh? Everyone loves her."

He let silence settle in as she sat there and breathed, making no move to do any kind of work.

"They're not very forthcoming, are they?" he said, again working a casualness he didn't feel into the question. "All questions. No answers."

She finally turned her head to look at him. "Did they ask you questions?"

"A few. And gave me a warning not to go anywhere."

Her eyebrows rose. "Are you a suspect?"

"I believe the detective's exact words were everyone is."

Zara frowned over that. "Hazeleigh shouldn't be. And they don't treat me like one. Thomas says the detective is great, but… Why are they taking things of Hazeleigh's? Why are they focusing on her? She's as likely to kill someone as…I don't know, Mother Teresa."

"So why do you look so worried?"

"That detective? She said Hazeleigh is keeping something from her."

"Is she?"

Zara stared at him, as if deciding why they were having this conversation. She chewed on her bottom lip, which drew his gaze to her mouth. Which was *not* acceptable, so he looked out at the mountains again.

In the end, she didn't answer his question or keep talking about the case, like he'd hoped. She changed the subject.

"I might need to take the afternoon off. I'm handling all the funeral arrangements. I just had to…do something this morning. Get out here. Breathe."

"If you need any help with anything, let me know."

"Help?"

"Sure. It can't be easy to make those kinds of arrangements. I can make a phone call or pick up flowers or whatever funerals entail. To lighten the load."

"Lighten the load," she echoed, staring at him like he'd slapped her, all the while speaking a foreign language.

"Yeah. It's called being friendly. Or maybe around here you call it being neighborly. I'm sure you've got family, neighbors, friends. But we're right here, so if you need something, you only have to ask."

She just kept staring at him, eyes wide and arrested. Like he'd just admitted to murdering and burying her sister.

Then she did the most incomprehensible thing he'd ever seen.

She started sobbing.

Chapter Five

Zara couldn't say it was the worst moment of her life. She'd seen her sister dead beneath the earth. She'd witnessed her mother's slow, agonizing death from cancer when she'd been a child. There had been a lot of bad days, so this didn't rank.

But never had she burst into tears in front of…anyone. Especially a virtual stranger.

When has anyone ever offered to lighten the load?

Not in a very long time. She gave the reins a tug and turned Sam around, then urged him into a run. Back to the stables. Away from Jake.

It was a temporary escape. Jake would follow her, and knowing his type, would poke and prod until she explained her little outburst.

Quite frankly, she knew embarrassment was silly. He'd say what he kept saying. Her sister had died. She deserved some time off. Some time to grieve. Crying wasn't beyond the pale. Apparently that's what normal people did.

Zara didn't know how to be normal. And she didn't know how to deal with someone like Jake. Everyone in her life had pretty much always been there. Wilde didn't change, which meant *she* didn't change. At least in the eyes of the people who knew her.

But Jake didn't look at her quite the same way everyone else did. None of those Thompson brothers did.

So why are you focusing on Jake?

She reached the stables. She didn't have the time or energy to think about Jake. She swung off the horse. Unfortunately she couldn't just bolt because she had to take care of Sam.

The wind had dried most of her tears. No doubt she looked a little worse for the wear, but she'd be fine once Jake caught up. She'd shrug it off and move on with her day.

Far away from *him*.

She started to unsaddle Sam. She didn't get very far before Jake appeared and swung off his horse.

There was a natural grace in the movement, like he'd been doing it his whole life, even though she knew he hadn't been. God knows he'd been awkward and stiff when she'd first started teaching the brothers how to ride a horse. But Jake and Landon had taken to the horses easily and quicker than the other three who could ride.

Jake even wore the cowboy hat like he'd been born on a ranch, not raised in the city. Like he was a pro at changing himself into whatever he needed to be.

She frowned at him.

"Stop scowling at me. I didn't mean to make you cry."

"That's not why I'm frowning at you," she muttered, turning her attention back to her horse. "And *you* didn't make me cry. I was just...overwhelmed."

"Clearly."

"It's kind of you—" it sounded like an accusation, even to her own ears. She tried to soften her words "—to offer to help. It caught me off guard."

"You don't have to explain it away. I fully expect anyone to have a few crying jags while going through what you're going through."

Anyone. Not any *woman*. Well, he knew how to step carefully, didn't he?

But she realized this was all about…her issues. Because she'd been waiting for the censure she was used to. The rolled eyes and heavy sighs that her father would have given her.

Toughen up, Zara. One of you has to.

"I don't know why kindness would catch you off guard. Aren't small-town folk used to rallying around when the going gets tough, with all types of kindness?"

"Wilde does rally," Zara said, insulted on her small town's behalf. They did. It was just different for her. She was the strong one. "But you're not Wilde. You're just some guy who bought my…" She'd been about to say "legacy" in the snottiest way she could, but that hardly repaid his kindness. "…family's ranch."

"In spite of that, you've taught us how to do all this." He spread his arm around to encompass the whole ranch even though they were inside the stables.

"Sure, but you're pay—"

"Yes, I know we've paid you for it and well, but you are a good teacher," he said, sounding impatient and firm. "To six men who hadn't had to be *taught* anything in a long time. To six men who bought your birthright out from under you, without your say in the matter. You were hard on us, but fair. You didn't *have* to be. You even handled Dunne's silences and Landon's endless jokes. What I'm trying to say, Zara, is we appreciate what you did for us, and continue to do. If we can help you, we will. We're...friends."

Friends.

God, she could use a friend. One who offered to *do* things. Even if she'd never take him up on it, the idea that he might pick up a flower arrangement or make a call was...

Flattening.

Zara did not want to be flattened.

"I don't know what to say to that," she muttered, closing Sam's stable door and stepping away from the man standing too close as he did the same.

He studied her, those blue eyes a distraction all on their own. Then add the cowboy hat and stubborn jaw and dark stubble...

He smiled, and it was kind, but there was something more than kind that lurked in his eyes. She didn't want to know what it was.

"You say thanks. That's it."

She shifted on her feet, wholly nonplussed by the effect he had on her. "Fine. Thanks."

He chuckled, slapped her on the shoulder like they were *buddies*. Yes, she was quite used to *that* treatment from men.

But then his hand stayed there, gave her shoulder a little squeeze. She assumed that was the sort of sorry-your-sister-died-and-we-found-the-body gesture a man like Jake made.

But his hand...lingered. And Zara didn't have the

first rightly clue what to do with *that*, and when she heard footsteps approaching, she only knew she had to step away from his hand.

When Thomas appeared in the stable entrance, she was glad she had.

"Sorry to interrupt," Thomas said, studying Jake with some suspicion. A suspicion Zara found she didn't care for.

But that was silly.

"We just need to go over the…site again. You guys can keep working. I'll act as go-between if we need anything else. I just wanted to let you know a few county guys would be out and about."

"Thanks," Zara said in unison with Jake. Because he was the property owner. Not her. It didn't just feel unfair in the moment. It felt wrong. Amberleigh pulled from the dirt—Hart dirt—but it wasn't even theirs anymore.

"I have to go to town. Talk to the Thompsons if you need anything," she said, desperately working to keep the tears out of her voice.

She'd cried enough. Now it was time to get something accomplished.

ZARA SCURRIED OUT of the stables, leaving Jake standing there under the narrowed gaze of her cousin. Thomas Hart wasn't wearing his uniform this morning. He was dressed in jeans and a sweatshirt, a ball cap pulled low on his head.

Jake tried to push away his distaste for cops, because this was Zara's cousin, and he was clearly here not in any official capacity but in an attempt to make things easier for his cousins. Jake couldn't be hard on that.

Not when Zara had fallen apart at the smallest offer of help. Like no one ever reached out and did anything for her.

He rocked back on his heels when Thomas didn't disappear. "No autopsy reports yet?"

"No."

And, well, since he had a cop here, why not ask? "Any timeline on that?"

"Why? Worried you'll need to disappear?"

"I don't have anything to hide," Jake said, making his smile wide and maybe a little sarcastic. Especially since it was a lie. He had plenty to hide. Just none of it had to do with the dead woman on his property.

"Neither of those girls had any trouble before you and your brothers showed up."

Jake kept his voice mild, though his temper stirred. "Zara said she hadn't seen her sister since she was sixteen and ran away. Sounds like trouble enough."

Thomas didn't have a quick rejoinder for that.

"Look, you can keep trying to tie me to this, but I didn't know any of those women before I, along with my brothers, bought the place from their old man. We handled everything through brokers."

"And isn't that fishy?"

"Not where I'm from."

"Well, it is here. And that does bring up a pretty interesting question. Just where *are* you from? Because you and your brothers don't seem to be from anywhere."

"You really think I killed this girl I don't know anything about, buried her on my own property, then dug her up in front of her sisters?" Never let it be said that Jake didn't know how to sidestep a question he didn't intend to answer.

Ever.

Thomas sighed, much like Zara had not that long ago. A slow sagging of the shoulders, regret, followed by shoring it all back up. "No, I don't really think that, but, boy, would it make my life a hell of a lot easier."

For the first time, Jake felt a glimmer of kindness toward the man. At least he could admit when he was wrong, much like Zara often did. "I can see the family resemblance. Zara can't lie either. The truth comes out in the same frustrated fashion."

Thomas slowly turned and fixed Jake with a speculative stare. "Just what kind of relationship do you have with my cousin?" He crossed his arms over his chest.

Jake tried not to scowl. So instead he half smiled. Maybe a little meanly. "Which one?"

Thomas sighed and looked up at the ceiling, filled with frustration and exhaustion. A look Jake remembered on quite a few foster parents' faces.

Too much work, this one.

But this was hardly about *him*.

"Look. Consider this a friendly warning. Zara isn't half as strong as she pretends to be. And Hazeleigh isn't half as weak as she pretends to be. Neither of them are as alone or defenseless as they might appear. So watch your step."

"They don't need defenses. Zara's been good to us when she didn't have any reason to be beyond a paycheck. I only want to repay her for that."

"Then stay out of the way of this investigation."

Jake kept his mouth firmly shut, because he wasn't so sure that was something he could do.

Thomas's phone rang and he frowned at the screen, immediately lifting it to his face. "What's up?" he answered.

He turned away from Jake quickly, but not before Jake saw the color in his face drain away. "You can't..." He took long strides out of the stables, but Jake followed. Silently, carefully. So Thomas wouldn't know he was within eavesdropping distance.

"Laurel," Thomas said. "Hazeleigh didn't kill anyone. I don't care what the evidence says."

Damn. They were going to arrest Hazeleigh. It would kill Zara. He glanced to where she'd gone. Her truck was still parked in front of the cabin, so she hadn't taken off yet. He'd need to stop her.

But he wanted to hear what else Thomas had to say.

"I know it's a conflict of interest if I arrest her, but I have to be there. She didn't do this. Surely we can put it—"

Thomas didn't speak, he just listened to whatever the detective said and then hung up.

Jake figured there was no point in pretending he didn't know what was going on. "Want me to go get Zara before she takes off?"

Thomas blew out a breath as he turned, somewhat incredulous that Jake was standing there. He looked like he was about to read Jake the riot act, then just slumped. "It'd be better coming from family."

"Nah, she's likely to kill the messenger." Bad choice

of words. "She can punch me and not feel guilty about it later. You'll need to be with Hazeleigh, I suspect."

Thomas swore. "This is a mess," he muttered. "All right, I'm going to meet the arresting cops over at Hazeleigh's work. Do everything you can to keep Zara here and not rushing down to the station. She'll only make matters worse. I'll call with lawyers I can recommend. Keep her here until I do."

"Got it."

"I sure hope you're her friend, Thompson. Because she's going to need one."

Chapter Six

Zara sat down at the kitchen table and made herself a list. They were almost out of milk. She supposed she needed to speak to the pastor at church. She didn't know how to plan a funeral, and she supposed she couldn't, really, until the body was released.

Body. Amberleigh.

She closed her eyes. Just for a second. Just to center herself. Find that well of strength she'd been building since she was a little girl. Because when there was no one else to be strong, it had to be her.

I can make a phone call or pick up flowers or whatever funerals entail. To lighten the load.

Jake had said that so sincerely. So offhandedly. As if it was just what people did. And maybe in his world that was the case. Zara wasn't sure she wanted to be part of that world. If she didn't handle everything, wouldn't that foundation of strength just dissolve away? Wouldn't she endlessly be leaning on people who would inevitably die, disappear, withdraw?

She stared at the little scrap of paper where she'd written *milk* and *church*.

Milk and *church*.

Suddenly those words didn't make any sense. A knock on her door even less sense, but it gave her something to do. She grabbed her keys and her phone. Whoever it was, she'd tell them she was on her way out.

Because she was. She had things to do.

She opened the front door and frowned at Jake standing there. "Are you following me around?" she asked, feeling...tired. Just completely exhausted by this constant parade of people.

"Actually, Thomas asked me to bring you some news."

She wanted to shut the door in his face. She didn't want news. She didn't want *Jake* to deliver it. "Why didn't he tell me himself?"

"He had to go... Listen, they're going to arrest Hazeleigh. He wanted to be there."

She appreciated the bluntness of it. Just rip off the bandage. Land the blow.

Arrest.

She laughed. The sound bubbled up and out of her. It was *insanity*.

Jake's eyebrows furrowed. "That wasn't a joke, Zara."

She shook her head. "No. Not at all." The laughter slowly morphed into something else. Something closer to panic and hysteria and she wasn't sure she could *breathe*. But if they were going to arrest Hazeleigh...

"I have to get to the fort. I have to be with her. Maybe I can—"

Jake stepped inside her cabin. *Her* cabin, blocking her way.

"Thomas asked me to keep you here," he said very

seriously. All tall and imposing body, blocking her door. *Her door.*

She looked at him. It wasn't shock that rocked through her. That was too simple. It was a mix of everything. The grief. The fury. The surprise. The horror. It all rose up, tied together and turned into a blinding rage that had no target.

So, she made him one. She swung and he narrowly grabbed her fist before it connected with his face. "Nice," he said, as if he was actually impressed.

"I *have* to get to Hazeleigh," she said between clenched teeth, trying to find her center of calm. That place inside her that always solved the problems, took control. Then she realized he was still holding her clenched fist.

She wrenched her hand out of his grasp. Her breath was coming in gasps and she supposed she should be grateful he'd stopped her before she could actually break his nose. It wasn't his fault… It wasn't…

She took two full steps back from him, lingering just a shade too close, like he'd physically stop her from leaving…or hug her if she fell apart again.

No, she wasn't going to fall apart. Couldn't let herself. Not again.

"I can't let her be alone."

"Thomas is going to be there. He said he'll call with a list of lawyers. Your cousin is going to look out for her."

"But she…" Zara swallowed. "You don't understand. Hazeleigh…" She couldn't say it. Couldn't tell him that her sister simply couldn't *handle* this.

"I've got something to show you."

"Jake—"

"Just follow me. Let me show you something, and then I'll drive you down to wherever they're holding Hazeleigh. Interfering isn't going to help. Don't you think Thomas knows what he's talking about?"

She tried to focus her scattered thinking. What was best for Hazeleigh? That's what she had to think about.

Not being arrested.

Could she beat the cops to Hazeleigh? Could she call and warn Hazeleigh? She knew Thomas would do what was best and right—within the *law*. But Zara didn't really care about the law when it came to her fragile, skittish sister. Ever since her last boyfriend had done a number on her, men in general had made her more uncomfortable than even her usual shy demeanor.

She jerked her chin to the door, a nonverbal sign she would follow him. Even though she had no plans to. He stepped outside and she locked up her cabin—something she wouldn't normally do, but with police crawling around happily arresting Hazeleigh, it seemed pretty imperative.

Jake started walking for the big house. Zara eyed her truck. How much space between them would she need?

"I wouldn't," he said blandly without even looking back at her.

Zara stopped where she was, keys clutched in her hand. "Or what?"

He turned and smiled at her, a little wolfishly. It felt a bit like they were in a Wild West standoff, ten paces apart, waiting to draw their weapons.

"I told Thomas I'd keep you here, so I intend to do

it. I'd be honor bound to stop you from getting in your truck."

She narrowed her eyes, studied him, trying to figure out how she could metaphorically outdraw him. He was a big guy, but she'd seen him move around the past month. He could be quick when he wanted to be. He'd be stronger than her—that was just fact. She was sure she could get past him if she had the time to figure out *how*. But she didn't.

And there was something about the way he said "honor bound" that made her reluctant to test him— when she was usually happy to test anyone. Anywhere.

"Give her a call if it'll make you feel better, but I can't let you go anywhere right now. I can show you something that might…help."

"Help? How?"

He raised an eyebrow at her. A clear gesture that she needed to just do what he said if she wanted to find out.

Zara inhaled and exhaled, slowly, carefully. It was the only way to make a decision when the world was falling apart around you. Breathe. Center. Focus.

She called Hazeleigh. First and foremost, she at least had to warn her sister what was coming. But when Hazeleigh answered, her voice was strained.

"I can't talk right now, Zee," Hazeleigh said, her voice faint.

"Haze, Thomas said they're going to arrest you. You need to—"

"Please don't worry about me. I can handle this."

Zara wanted to ask "since when," but she didn't say anything because Hazeleigh had already hung up.

Zara's fingers tightened around the phone. It took

her long, ticking seconds to pull it away from her face. To accept the reality.

Hazeleigh didn't want her help. Oh sure, when Douglas had been harassing her, she'd needed help, but now that she was getting *arrested*, she could handle things.

Zara thought about what the detective had said. That Hazeleigh was hiding something. Hazeleigh was never hiding anything. Not from Zara. But...

"Come on, Zara," Jake said, a gentle note to his voice she wanted to soften against. So she did the opposite. Straightened her spine and leveled him with a cool glare.

"Fine. Lead the way." She'd go see what he had to show her, and it would give her time to come up with a plan.

JAKE WAS A little surprised when she actually followed him, walking across the long expanse between cabin and house. Despite her much shorter legs, she kept pace with him. She often did.

He'd half expected her to bolt for the truck and fight him. Half expected he'd be forced to stop her. But she'd sized him up and clearly decided she couldn't manage it.

That didn't mean he trusted her not to try it at some other point. In fact, he wouldn't be surprised if she was just lulling him into complacency. She'd be disappointed. But he gave her credit for strategic thinking.

He'd have to be a little strategic here too. It wouldn't be easy, because Zara was no easy mark. She would question everything. Including his motives.

Complicated, that.

She moved onto the porch before him, reaching out to open the door. Then she stopped herself, something arresting and painful crossed over her face.

Then she stepped back.

For over a month this woman had taught him and his "brothers" to ranch, with steely glares and snappy commands but always a certain kind of fairness. A dry humor. There'd been a seriousness, a graveness to the way she taught them how to tend *her* land.

But he'd never seen the emotion slam into her in quite that fashion. Realizing this wasn't her home anymore.

For the first time, Jake deeply regretted everything that had brought them here.

She gestured at the door. "Guess I shouldn't go barging in. Who knows what six single men living together do in the privacy of their own home."

"Fantasizing about it a bit, huh?"

She let out a little huff of a laugh, like he'd hoped, but it didn't lighten the gravity on her face.

He opened the door, led her inside. She looked around like she was stepping into a dollhouse or a snow globe. Maybe a play set. Like it wasn't quite real.

"It's upstairs," he said, forcing himself to stop watching all her expressions, all her emotions. He'd brought her here to take her mind off Hazeleigh and it certainly looked like he'd succeeded.

She followed him up the stairs and he didn't look behind him as he strode through the narrow hallway. It struck him in the moment that she would have walked up and down this hallway as a child. A little girl.

Zara as a little girl was hard to imagine. He couldn't imagine her as anything but just the same, only smaller.

"No Christmas decorations?"

He found the lie he'd told the detective didn't roll off the tongue. "One of the things six single men living together don't really get around to doing." He stepped into his bedroom and, when she followed, closed the door behind him.

"Eyes closed for a second," he said.

Her eyebrows rose. "Is this where you kill me, laugh and say it was you all the time?"

He gave her a baleful glance. "If that's what you want to think." They stood in another kind of stand-off and he waited. Since he kept all the things no one could ever find in the same place, he wasn't about to give her the ammunition.

He could have left her downstairs, but it was too likely one of his brothers would walk in and demand answers he wasn't planning on giving just yet.

After an interminable silence and refusal to blink on her part, she finally heaved out a sigh. "Fine. What-ever."

She turned and faced the door. He couldn't tell if she was closing her eyes, but as long as she was faced away, she wouldn't be able to see the intricate system of locks and codes that kept all his private information private.

He finished unlocking the door and opened the small walk-in closet to what he'd been working on the past few days. He slid his personal things to the side, hiding them behind a large bureau...which also hid things. He flipped over some of the pictures he wouldn't want her to have to see, on the big board of information he'd made.

"All right. You can look."

She turned and stepped over to where he stood. Her expression was skeptical and wary, but no, not afraid.

Either she trusted him in particular or she was too trusting in general. The latter made him feel fiercely protective. Which was funny since she was the type of woman who would be offended at the very thought.

She frowned at the board he'd been putting together. His very own nonmilitary military campaign. Maybe the cops would figure it out first, but that didn't mean he couldn't do his due diligence.

"What is…? You're investigating." Her dark eyebrows were drawn together, lines dug into her forehead. Her braid wasn't as tightly wound today, as if she hadn't had the energy to twist her hair into control.

She just stared. She reached out and touched the timeline he'd written out with what he knew.

He had blanks. Quite a few. She could probably fill a lot of them.

"I don't understand. How'd you put all this together?"

"Let's just say… I have a special set of skills."

"Or you've watched too many *CSI* television shows," she muttered, but her gaze took in everything. The timelines, the pictures he hadn't flipped over. "I asked the wrong question. *Why* did you put this all together?"

"None of this has sat right. I just thought if I tried to make sense of it, put the information together, I might be able to see something the cops don't."

She took that in, seemed to absorb the words as she

scanned all the information on his makeshift board. Then she turned to him slowly, and it seemed she had a particularly difficult time dragging her gaze from the board.

But eventually she pinned him with one of her accusatory glares. "Why do you care? Don't tell me it's a kindness. Don't lie to me. Why would you go through all this trouble?"

He was getting a little tired of her casual accusations. "I didn't kill your sister."

She huffed out a frustrated breath. "I know that. But you're hiding…something with all this." She waved at the board. "Why is everyone *hiding* something?"

And he found he wanted to tell her. All the truths he'd sworn to tell no one. He didn't know why. The way she impatiently and easily believed he didn't kill Amberleigh—even though she knew next to nothing about him. The way she seemed to march through life, being so sure of her place in it, even when her place had been uprooted.

How she wanted to swoop in and save Hazeleigh when there was no way to do it. That wouldn't stop her. He knew that.

But wanting something and doing something were two very different things.

"Let's just say it's in my best interest if there aren't a bunch of people poking around the Thompson brothers' lives. *Not* because we've done anything wrong. I know you suspect we did, or we're up to something. But it's nothing like that."

"Then what's it like?"

"I can't tell you that." He gestured at the board. "But

the way I see it, we can work together because we have the same endgame in mind. You want to clear Hazeleigh. I want to get this taken care of and away from us. They've arrested Hazeleigh, and I think we both know she's no murderer. Which means someone has to figure out who is, because if the cops are focused on her, they aren't focused on what really happened."

Zara stared at the board again. She was faintly shaking her head back and forth, but she was thinking. Considering. He could see that easily enough.

So, he pressed. "I know you could fill in these blanks. So could people in town. So could some deeper research, but if we pool what you know and what I know about solving a problem, I think we can get Hazeleigh out of this mess without causing much of a fuss."

"That depends, doesn't it?"

"On what?"

"On who really killed Amberleigh. Because she didn't die out wherever she ran away to. She died here and recently." Zara shook her head. "Which means the chances of this being a stranger are low. And the chances of Hazeleigh hiding something, like the detective said, are high." She blew out a breath, still shaking her head. "Do you honestly think you can figure out who did this with…this?"

"Yeah, I do."

Chapter Seven

Zara knew a thing or two about false hope. About putting your faith into *words* and *promises*. Dad used to make those. Eventually she'd stopped believing and he'd stopped promising.

But she so desperately wanted to believe in *this*. It was work after all. Compiling the information. The evidence. The pictures. But a few were facedown against the board. She reached out to remove the magnet so she could flip them over.

"What are these?"

His hand flew out and stopped her. The gentleness of the way his fingers closed over hers at odds with the sudden, certain movement of his hand reaching out at all. He cleared his throat uncomfortably. "I got some pictures of the…scene of the crime. You don't want to see it again, Zara."

No, she supposed she didn't. She let her hand fall.

"How?"

"Best if you don't ask 'how' too much."

She truly didn't know what to do with this. *Any* of it. "I can't let Hazeleigh sit in jail. I can't…" He had put together all the facts he had about the case. Like a cop might. "We should show this to…" She trailed off, thinking of her cousin. Who was a good guy, but a cop. Someone who had to play by the rules.

Jake…wouldn't. She didn't buy his whole *innocent* routine exactly, though no matter how she tried to convince herself he was hiding something terrible, she couldn't quite believe that of him. She supposed women got fooled all the time by charming or even sometimes not-so-charming men who said they were harmless.

But that was it. She didn't think Jake was *harmless*. Certainly not that steely way he'd eyed her and very easily, gently and *seriously* warned her not to try and make a run for her truck. She didn't think he was even particularly honest all the time.

She just thought there was something…decent about him. He wasn't going to let bad things happen.

She sighed. She was going to be the woman who fell for "I've got a secret I can't tell you, but I swear it's for your own good."

And honestly, she was too tired to care. Here was someone offering something she wanted. An attempt at answers—that weren't the wrong ones like Hazeleigh being a murderer. Even if she *was* hiding something.

"So, what now?"

"You fill in some blanks for me. Then I'll take you down to talk to Hazeleigh, and you'll see if you can get her to tell you what she's hiding."

"And then what?"

"Those are today's steps. We get those tasks accomplished, then tomorrow, we'll work on next steps."

It sounded so reasonable. It sounded like action and

a plan. So, she pointed at his timeline and started to fill it in for him.

"It was August when Amberleigh ran away. The summer we were sixteen. Right before school started."

"No one seems too keen on talking about *why*."

"No, they wouldn't." She wasn't. She could remember all too well the aftermath of what Amberleigh had done. She didn't want to bring it up now. Not when Amberleigh was dead. An unbidden image of her face in the ground had Zara closing her eyes in pain.

Yes, she thought her sister had been dead a long time, but that grief had never gone away. Now it was stronger, sharper, because there was no hope left.

Without hope, a person had to cling to hard work and the truth. So, she'd have to tell him. No matter what it made Jake think of Amberleigh.

"She disappeared the same day as a man twice her age. A man who was very well loved, very much respected and very married. It was a shock to everyone—not just that he'd have an illegal affair with a teenager, one of his daughter's friends, but that he'd then just up and leave town."

Jake frowned. "Isn't that the kind of thing people would love to gossip about?"

"Sure, when it was fresh. Not so gleeful when the girl they blamed is dead. Small towns aren't perfect, but Wilde loves its own. At least when they're murdered."

Jake seemed to think this over. He offered no commentary. Just wrote some things down on his board. "And this man isn't a suspect?"

"I suppose he is. We wouldn't know, would we? But no one's been able to find him. Either of them.

My family tried to find Amberleigh, but we only had so many resources. The Phillips family was and is one of the richest families in town. I know Mr. Phillips's daughter spent years trying to track him down. Trying to figure out what happened. But he was never seen or heard from again. It's been ten years."

"And you never heard from or saw Amberleigh again?"

"No."

"What about Hazeleigh?"

"No." But a strange feeling skittered up her spine. Because the detective's words kept echoing in Zara's head. *But she's hiding something. I'd encourage her to tell me. Sooner rather than later.* And how unsurprised Hazeleigh seemed to be about being arrested, insisting on the phone she could handle it, when Hazeleigh was never known for her handling of anything.

She ran away, or avoided, or left Zara to handle it. Maybe that wasn't the fairest assessment of her sister, but she wasn't feeling particularly fair right now.

"Zara?"

Her first instinct was to push it away. To never speak word of her doubts. Certainly not to a stranger, but she couldn't stop looking at the board. The time and effort it had taken. Sure, he was doing it for himself—to get the cops away from sniffing around him and his brothers—but it was still time and effort.

"Hazeleigh never saw or talked to Amber that I know of."

"But you're wondering if she did without you knowing?"

"I really don't know. I never dreamed Hazeleigh

was keeping something from me. Never in a million years, but the past day… It's all I can think." And it felt awful. Like a betrayal, but no amount of talking herself out of suspicion could make that little worm of a feeling go away.

"Well, maybe she'll tell you what it is now that she's in some serious trouble."

Zara managed a smile, though she knew it frayed at the edges. Because if Hazeleigh was keeping something from her, she was already in the serious trouble.

JAKE GOT ZARA to answer a few more questions he hadn't been able to surmise or pick up from town gossip. She looked like a ghost of herself, standing there in front of the board of information. Pale, still gripping her bag like it was a lifeline.

But she didn't fall apart. She didn't cry like she had this morning. She gave him the answers, a lot of time in a rather monotone voice, her gaze never leaving the board.

"Do you really think you can put all this together? I mean, I assume the police are working with the same information."

"I assume. Hopefully, if they are, they let Hazeleigh go as soon as possible. Unless they're barking up the Hazeleigh tree, one we both know is wrong, because it's convenient."

"Thomas might have to follow the letter of the law and allow Hazeleigh to be arrested, but he knows she's not a murderer. He won't just let them keep focusing on her."

"Unless he doesn't have a choice."

She frowned at that but didn't argue with him.

The door to his room burst open, and Landon stood there in nothing but a towel held around his waist, dripping wet.

"Jake, damn it, where the hell is the—oh." He cleared his throat, looked from Zara to Jake with some amusement, then grinned at Zara. "Well, hi."

Zara's eyebrows rose, but that was about her only reaction to a half-naked man standing in the doorway. Jake supposed he was lucky Landon had bothered with a towel.

"Where's the soap you were supposed to pick up this morning?" Landon asked, apparently having no qualms about dripping all over the floor or standing there in nothing but a towel.

"I haven't made it to town yet. I'm going out in a minute. Why don't you go put some pants on since there's a guest in our house?"

"Oh, I didn't mind," Zara said with just a little *too* much feeling and a sweet smile Landon's way to boot.

Which earned a grin from Landon and a scowl from Jake, though he couldn't say why it bothered him she should be…ogling.

"You can *go* now," Jake said pointedly at Landon.

"Touchy, touchy," Landon said with a grin Jake knew meant he would be getting razzed later. Landon finally turned and left, but Jake didn't watch him. He watched Zara *watch* him.

"Sorry about that," he grumbled, irritable for reasons he didn't want to analyze.

Zara was staring at the little puddle Landon had left behind. "The interruption or the strip show?"

"Both."

"I don't mind a show."

She had taken him off guard and so he could only stare at her, probably gaping a bit. She shrugged.

"You and your brothers aren't ogres, Jake. And, no matter what anyone might think, I *am* a woman. I enjoy a six-pack and impressive thighs."

"All right," he muttered, wanting as far out of this conversation as he could get. ASAP. He began closing up the board, locking up the closet.

"Nice shoulders are good too, and—"

"I said *all right*," he ground out, giving her a quelling glare.

She laughed. And it was hard to stay all tense and uncomfortable when she did. Not just because she was in the middle of something horrible and it was nice to be able to bring her some relief to that, but because she'd been pretty serious ever since they'd arrived. He knew she had a sense of humor. It usually came out cutting and snarky. But this was a sort of wicked delight.

"I'll drive you into town and see what's what at the police station. If they let you talk to Hazeleigh, I'll go run my errands, then pick you up when I'm finished. Sound good?"

She nodded. "I feel it's probably a waste of time to point out I could drive myself."

"Then it's just as equally a waste of time to point out I'm going to town anyway, and you might as well take an offer of help when it's made."

She stared at him for a second or two longer than was comfortable. "All right," she murmured. Still staring at him, with dark brown eyes that…

He turned away abruptly. "So, let's get going."

She followed him out into the hallway. "How'd you pick your rooms?" she asked, and when he looked back at her, she was studying the upstairs. "Who got what?"

"We just walked through, picked what felt best suited to our needs. Dunne's downstairs because of his leg. Henry's in that outbuilding that has a bed, because he's a grumpy SOB. Then the last four of us are up here."

"Why did that room suit your needs?"

He shrugged, uncomfortable with the line of questioning but knowing her and life well enough not to show any discomfort. "I don't know. Had a nice view out the window."

They went down the stairs, Zara strangely silent behind him. When they reached the main floor he turned to look at her. "What?"

She inhaled, exhaled, still studying him in that way that made him want to fidget. When he'd been stared at and inspected and yelled at by so many superior officers and never so badly wanted to look away.

"It was mine," she said quietly. "So was that bureau in the closet. Let me guess. You have something you wouldn't want anyone to see hidden in that false bottom?"

It was such a shock, and he knew it shouldn't have been. But it had been a while since someone had gotten the best of him—and the last time had been an entire terrorist organization. Not a pretty rancher in small-town Wyoming.

Because yes, he had a few things hidden in that false bottom.

She sailed by him. This had once been her house and she knew the way after all. "We can talk about it on the way to the police department."

Chapter Eight

Zara savored the shocked look on Jake's face all the way to the police station. He was usually so...composed. She hadn't fully realized that. He did it with an ease and casualness that was easily mistaken as a happy-go-lucky kind of guy.

But there was a deeper current running under Jake's facade. Once she'd finally broken through it, she could look back and see all the ways he'd employed that facade.

And wasn't it disappointing that she was thinking more about that than Landon's impressive shoulders?

She sat in the passenger seat of the car and mostly kept her gaze on the windshield in front of her. But occasionally her gaze strayed to Jake's profile. He'd carefully hidden his shock and discomfort. His hand on the wheel was relaxed. His jaw wasn't tense and his shoulders lounged back against the driver's seat.

But there was something in his very, *very* intense gaze on the road ahead of him that Zara had the sneaking suspicion was all those *feelings* he was trying to hide.

"So. I guess you're not hiding any murder weapons in the false bottom."

His blue gaze flicked to hers, briefly, but there was a telling jerk of surprise in that almost-nothing move.

"No."

"But something?"

His gaze was back on the road, but his jaw had tensed some. "Sure. We all have secrets, don't we?"

She thought about the detective saying Hazeleigh was hiding something. Zara thought of her own life. Did she have secrets? Not the kind a person hid in false bottoms—at least, now that she didn't keep an adolescent journal full of ridiculously embarrassing thoughts she'd had the good sense to burn after Amberleigh had found it and read it aloud to her friends when they'd been thirteen.

But the man next to her—as helpful as he was being—certainly had bigger secrets than crushes, childish slights and pubescent, overemotional worries.

The kind of secrets he didn't want the *police* poking around.

Common sense told her she shouldn't trust him. Not a man so obviously trying to hide something. But underneath all that sense—she had a...gut feeling, her great-grandfather would have called it. It told her that while Jake might have secrets, he wasn't *dangerous*.

At least, not to her.

Jake pulled his truck into a parking space at the police station and dread iced her insides. She didn't want to handle this. She didn't want to face an *arrested* Hazeleigh. Or whatever her sister was hiding from her.

Worse, she didn't want to go in there only to be turned away. Would they even let her see Hazeleigh? Or would she be completely shut out?

Nothing like a situation with no good outcome.

Amberleigh's face in the dirt drifted into her mind and she squeezed her eyes shut in an effort to push it away.

She felt the gentle pressure of Jake's hand touching her arm through the sleeve of her coat.

"Do you want me to go in with you?"

She shook her head, though she didn't lean away from his hand on her arm. It felt nice. Like something holding her up. Ballast.

Truth be told, she wanted some as she walked into the police station, but she had to be strong enough to do this on her own. "Thank you, but I feel like there might be some questions about why you drove me. Why you're getting involved. The kind of questions you're trying to avoid."

She opened her eyes, determined to be strong. In control. But Jake was staring at her with that *seriousness* she didn't know what to do with.

"I can handle a few questions," he said. Firmly. Certain. An offer of kindness at the cost of what he was trying to do.

It was a simple statement that landed with the strength of an avalanche. She'd thought earlier she didn't want to be flattened, but she was starting to wonder if she had a choice.

"I'll be fine," she managed to say. Because something about going in there with him as an anchor of sorts felt a lot more scary and dangerous than facing this herself. "Thanks. I'll text you if they won't let me see her." She got out of the truck and walked with purpose for the door.

She hesitated a moment before reaching out to open it. She glanced back, and he was sitting there. Watching her go in. Like he wouldn't leave until he was sure she was inside. Until he was certain she'd be able to do what she came for.

A lump formed in her throat. Old memories, being afraid, looking behind her, and no one being there. Because she was the strong one. The one who couldn't be afraid.

She cleared her throat and straightened her shoulders. Just because there was someone in that usual empty space didn't mean she could afford to be weak or afraid. She had to save Hazeleigh.

No one else would.

She stepped into the little entryway and waited to be buzzed in. She hadn't been in here for years. But back when they were sixteen, and Amberleigh had disappeared, she'd spent quite a bit of time in and out of the Bent County police station.

The receptionist smiled at her and offered a greeting, but the detective was walking down a staircase at the same time.

"Zara. Hi." She looked at the receptionist. "Sign in Zara Hart. No ID needed. I can confirm identity."

The receptionist nodded and pulled a clipboard toward her while the detective led Zara away.

"I guess you're here to see Hazeleigh."

"If I can."

Detective Delaney-Carson nodded, leading Zara up some stairs. "We can let you see her, but an officer will have to be in the room with you."

"Can it be Thomas?"

She smiled apologetically, and her eyes were kind. Not like so many of the officers they'd dealt with during Amberleigh's disappearance.

"I'm afraid not. Both because it'd be a conflict of interest and because he's on a call right now. He said he'd get you the name of some lawyers. I'd highly encourage you to find the right fit for you guys as soon as possible."

She led Zara down a hallway, another set of stairs. Then paused outside a gray metal door. She leaned in, her voice low and hushed.

"Thomas is adamant that your sister didn't do this. And I'm inclined to believe him. You might be his family, but he's a good cop and it doesn't feel like he's letting emotions cloud his instincts. But there is evidence against Hazeleigh. The kind we, as a police department, can't ignore. With evidence like that, we didn't have a choice in arresting her. But that doesn't mean, as the lead detective on this case, I won't keep looking for more evidence that proves a better theory."

Zara was slightly surprised at the detective's…kindness? Belief in Thomas? She thought of Jake's board. Would he have more information that could help the detective prove Hazeleigh didn't do it?

But all of those questions faded away as everything the detective said fully penetrated. There was *evidence*. Whatever they'd taken out of the cabin with the search warrant. "What kind of evidence?"

The detective sighed. "I'm sorry. I can't give you that information. However, if Hazeleigh knows what we took or what it is, she can tell you."

It was a hint of sorts. To ask Hazeleigh about it. "Thank you, detective."

She smiled thinly. "Call me Laurel. And you don't have to be polite to the person making your sister's life harder. I can take a little resentment. Part and parcel with the job."

Zara looked at the doorway. Hazeleigh was in there. Her life definitely harder. But it wasn't Laurel's fault. "I think I'll save all my bad manners for whoever is responsible."

The detective opened the door and nodded to the officer in the corner. "This is Zara Hart, Ms. Hart's sister." As if it wasn't obvious by the whole identical-faces thing, but maybe it was procedure. "When she's done, have someone escort her back out."

The officer nodded.

"Zara, if there's anything you want to talk to me about afterward, feel free to ask an officer to bring you to my office. Or you can call me. You still have my card?"

Zara nodded. Laurel gave her a reassuring pat on the shoulder. "I'll leave you to it."

Zara turned to face her sister. She sat at a table. She had handcuffs on her narrow wrists, and she had her hands clasped tightly in front of her on the table.

Zara felt brittle. Like if she moved, she might tremble and fall into a million pieces.

Hazeleigh attempted a smile. It faltered at the edges. "Everything is fine," she said, attempting a breezy tone that didn't fool Zara for a second.

"This is not fine," Zara managed. Her voice shook,

hopefully with conviction and not fear. She moved to take the seat across from Hazeleigh.

"Well, not ideal. But fine enough. I just have to sit here for now, and that detective comes in every so often to ask me questions. I don't know what's going to happen next. But that's okay. She said Thomas can come in and talk to me too, when he's not busy."

"How is that okay? How is any of this okay?"

Hazeleigh reached forward, paused when the guard said "no touching" in a curt, no-nonsense order. Hazeleigh put her cuffed hands in her lap.

"The detective said they have evidence," Zara said, hoping if she supplied *some* information, any of this might start to make sense.

Hazeleigh's forehead puckered. "Yes. They found some things in my room, but they aren't mine. Well, some of it is. It's sort of complicated."

"What is it? How is it complicated? I'm in the dark here, Hazeleigh. Why are you keeping me there?" Was she just confused because of shock and tragedy? Or…

"They found a sweater with some blood on it, and because Amberleigh's body…" Hazeleigh swallowed, and her eyes flickered with pain and grief and something that looked altogether too close to guilt. "She was shot in the same place the blood was. I told them I'd never seen it, of course, but they think I'm lying because…"

"Because why?"

"It was in a trash bag. Under my mattress."

Zara was sure the room spun. Something echoed in her ears and a pressure built in her chest. *"What?"*

she screeched. That wasn't just evidence. That was...
damning. Hidden, bloody clothes.

Hazeleigh gave her a censuring look, and it was just
as disorienting to have her sister be the calm, authoritative one while she panicked as it was to have Hazeleigh say a bloody sweater had been hidden under her
mattress.

A shrill sound echoed through the room, and Zara
nearly jumped a foot. She looked behind her at the
guard. He'd answered his cell phone and was speaking in low tones.

Distracted.

Zara leaned forward. "What aren't you telling me?"
she demanded in a whisper.

Hazeleigh whispered back, just as fervently. "Just
let it be, okay? Everything is fine. Really. I'm safest
right here."

"Safest?" As if her safety was in question. "Haze—"

"Leave it," Hazeleigh said. Firmly. As firm as she'd
ever said anything to Zara. In their entire lives. "Don't
go poking around looking for things. Let the detective
handle it. She seems nice."

She seems nice. "She had you arrested for murder.
Murder, Hazeleigh."

Hazeleigh leaned back with an odd coolness in her
gaze Zara had never seen out of her sister. Not in their
entire lives. "For my good. For yours. Let it be, Zaraleigh. Just let it be."

JAKE COMPLETED HIS errands for the house, did a little
casual asking around about Amberleigh. Townspeople's
theories on how she'd died, on why she'd run away.

Why she'd come back recently, without telling her sisters. It helped to canvas opinions. Put them together and try to pull a thread of truth out of them.

He hadn't found the thread yet, but he was working on it.

When Zara texted him that she was finished at the police station, he was already in the parking lot. A few minutes later, she stepped outside, blinked at the bright afternoon sunshine and then started toward him.

She looked…shell-shocked. A soldier not quite sure what she'd just stumbled out of. Alive and still intact on the outside, but forever changed on the inside.

Jake himself had to blink away old images superimposing themselves on Zara. Bloody men stumbling through chaos, and Zara walking through the center of it all.

But half that vision wasn't true. *Just your brain playing tricks on you: one, two, three, four, five. You are safe and here: five, four, three, two, one.*

By the time she reached his truck, the coping mechanisms had settled him. Whatever leftover anxiety he felt she wouldn't see because she was wrapped up in her own.

She sat in the seat, clutching her purse, frowning at the windshield.

"Buckle up, and we'll head home."

She didn't say anything. Didn't even acknowledge he'd spoken.

"That bad, huh?"

When she still didn't acknowledge him, he reached over the middle console and her body and grabbed the seatbelt himself. He pulled it across her and clicked it into place.

She finally moved, turning her head to stare at him. And because he was leaning over, their faces were rather close. Close enough to count her eyelashes. To notice the faint freckles on her nose and an even fainter scar above her dark eyebrows. To find his mind rendered utterly blank by the depth of her brown eyes.

Which was shock enough he forced himself to ease back, desperate for a little distance from the heaviness of whatever emotion moved through him. Besides, there were more important things at hand. "So, you saw her?"

Zara nodded slowly. "Yes."

"Did she tell you anything helpful?"

"No. Not exactly. I…" Zara blew out a breath and seemed to get some inner grip on herself. The dazed look went away, the odd stillness turned into a wave of small movements. Purposefully unclasping her hands from the purse, sitting back in the seat, crossing her ankles and then uncrossing them as she leaned forward. "She told me to leave it be. To not go poking around looking for things. That she was *safest* there." Zara looked out at the police station building.

"Safe. That's an odd choice of words."

"I thought so too. Why would jail be safe?" She shook her head. "Laurel, the detective, said she's still looking beyond Hazeleigh, but the evidence was damning enough they had to bring her in."

Jake pulled out of the parking spot. "Well, that's better than her thinking it's Hazeleigh, I suppose. But what kind of evidence would be so damning?"

"A bloody sweater hidden in her room. Hazeleigh said it wasn't hers, but… How else would it get under her mattress?"

"Someone's framing her."

Zara's eyebrows drew even closer together, a deep line running across her forehead. He wanted to ask her about the scar there and knew now was especially not the time. He needed to focus. On the situation. Not on *her*.

"Who? How?" She shook her head. "Too many questions and none of it makes sense. She told me to leave it be. Not to poke into anything. But what would you do if your sibling told you not to do something?" she asked, turning to him. Her eyes so…vulnerable. An odd twist of events for Ms. Hard-Ass Cowgirl.

"I don't have sib—" He realized his mistake too late. She raised her eyebrows, and then a look close to triumph crossed her face.

Because she'd finally caught him in that lie she'd been so sure they'd been telling.

"I was adopted," he said before she could accuse him of anything. It was always the story for when things didn't add up, and it wasn't so far from the truth as to be a lie. "When I was older, and they were. My brothers are my brothers, but it's different than identical triplets, I assume."

She frowned a little, that I-knew-it light fading from her eyes. "I suppose," she murmured, clearly not convinced. "But in *my* family, when you tell your sibling *not* to do something, it's like waving a red flag. Now it's all they want to do."

"So, you think she *wants* you to go poking around?"

he asked, glad they had this to focus on rather than sibling talk.

"I'm not sure. Part of me thinks she was sincere, but she wasn't herself. She was acting like…"

"Like?"

"…me." Zara shook her head. "Strong and in control. The leader. That's always me."

Jake thought that seemed kind of sad. Reminded him a bit of Cal. Always a little separate from the pack. Always so determined to be strong, even when they could use some help. As if they didn't know how to handle a life where they weren't the leaders, charging through the fray, fighting all the enemies.

"You know, Thomas said something to me…" Jake figured telling her cousin had said she wasn't as strong as she acted wasn't the best way to get through to her, so he kept that part to himself. "Hazeleigh isn't as fragile as you think."

Zara shook her head. "No offense, but I think I know my identical sister a little bit better than a few dudes. She needs help, and I'm the only one who's going to do it."

"What about your father?"

She moved, strangely almost like a flinch. She seemed not to know what to say to that. "Listen, let's just head back to the ranch. I've got some things to do."

"Like what? Poke around where Hazeleigh told you not to?"

She shrugged as he pulled his truck out of the police station parking lot.

"It denotes a kind of guilt, doesn't it? Don't poke

around. Leave things be. Why should I? Why shouldn't I know what happened to Amberleigh?"

"She said jail is the safest place for her. Maybe she's trying to protect you."

She bristled. "Well, I don't care if she is. If there's danger, then someone should figure it out to protect *her*."

"And that someone has to be you?"

"Apparently."

Jake frowned at the road. He didn't like the idea of Zara putting herself in danger, but he also knew the pointlessness of beating himself against the brick wall of someone who thought they had to be in charge of everything.

So, he'd just have to stick close. If she wanted to protect Hazeleigh, that was fine. But someone was damn well going to protect *her*.

"Okay. So, the cops already searched your place, but Hazeleigh doesn't want you poking around, which means there's more to find. Where would Hazeleigh hide something she didn't want you to poke around and find?"

"Work."

"So, let's go."

"Now? Jake, I really do appreciate your help, but I have my own truck. My own…two feet."

"'Course you do. But why only use two feet when four will get the job done faster?"

"It is on the way home anyway," she said with a nose wrinkle of distaste. "But I really don't need—"

"I didn't ask what you needed, Zara. I said we're going." And that was that.

Chapter Nine

It was a strange feeling in Zara's life to be railroaded by someone determined to help her. She didn't *like* it, because she didn't like anyone telling her what to do or deciding things about what she was going to do or whatever.

But it was hard to find a good argument when he wasn't taking over per se. He was mostly acting as chauffeur and what was wrong with that?

It felt like *something* should be, but she couldn't figure out whatever it was. So, she watched the world roll by. Back through Wilde. She instructed Jake to turn off before they got to the road that would lead them to the ranch.

He drove the back roads, following the small brown sign for Fort Dry. When he pulled into the park's lot, he stared dubiously at the sight before him.

Three small buildings huddled together, surrounded on three sides by a pretty white picket fence that Zara knew the park department painted every year. The landscape around the fort was nothing but flat snow-covered land, the mountains far off in the distance.

"This was a…fort?" Jake asked, sounding dubious.

"Someone inside will no doubt be quite happy to give you a history lesson, but yes. Fort Dry. It's a living-history thing. Hazeleigh works for the guy who runs it. She has a little office here, though she does most of her work at the library or at the cabin. But if she was hiding something, it'd be safest to hide it here."

But Zara didn't know what she'd be looking for. "I don't understand why she'd hide something from me. It makes *no* sense."

Jake's gave her shoulder a squeeze. "So let's go make sense of it."

Zara wasn't sure how to anticipate all those little touches. It seemed like second nature to him now. When for the past month he'd kept an easy distance. A *careful* distance.

But Jake had been there. Jake had been the first to dig up Amberleigh. She supposed that had to have been disorienting for him. Her and Hazeleigh's face in the dirt *and* right there in front of him.

"You don't have to…" She blew out a breath. She kept saying the same things to him, and yet, here they still were. No answers. Him still there.

Ballast.

"How about this? You stop telling me what I don't have to do, as I'm not at all afraid of saying the words *no* or *I'd rather not*. If I'm here, it's because I want to be. If I'm helping, it's because I want to be."

She wanted to ask him why, but she knew the answer, didn't she? He wanted to keep the cops off his proverbial doorstep. To hide whatever was in the false bottom of the bureau.

But that made *shoulder* touches a little unnecessary.

She marched forward, ignoring the odd pang inside her chest as Jake's hand slid off her shoulder. She bypassed the main building, hoping she'd avoid Mr. Field and anyone else so she wouldn't have to answer any questions or field any condolences.

But as she headed for the far building that housed Hazeleigh's office, Zara stopped on a dime. Even though the woman was dressed in historical clothing, a big, sweeping dress that went from her chin down to her toes, Zara recognized her immediately.

She also stopped dead in her tracks. And they stood there on the icy path staring at each other from a great distance.

Eventually, the woman broke the silence and the gap first.

Kate moved up to stand just a few feet away. "Zara. You... Um, hi."

Zara needed a minute to find her voice. "Kate. Hi."

"Hi."

They stared at each other in uncomfortable silence. Hazeleigh never mentioned Kate working here, though Zara knew it was true. Kate Phillips had become something they didn't talk about in their family. Just like Amberleigh.

Is that why Hazeleigh is hiding something from you? All those no-talk zones?

"I'm so sorry about Amberleigh," Kate said with feeling and kindness.

Years ago, Zara might have known what to do with it. Now, across a valley of accusations and bone-deep hurts, Zara didn't know what to say.

"The police came and asked me a few questions," Kate continued, standing there in clothes incongruous to the current time period, and yet Kate looked perfectly comfortable in them. She and Hazeleigh had always loved to dress up. "I told them everything I know."

Quite a few words, none of them kind, circled around Zara's brain. But Kate's gaze flicked to Jake behind Zara.

Zara had nearly forgotten about him. About why she was here. Because old hurts and pain had come back in the blink of an eye.

Apparently it was the week for that. "I just need to have a quick look around Hazeleigh's office."

Kate's gaze went from Jake back to Zara and she smiled thinly. "I was just locking it up. Mr. Field didn't want anyone messing with Hazeleigh's organization while she's…"

"In jail," Zara supplied for Kate. "Accused of murdering our sister."

Kate's face hardened. "Like I said, I told the police everything I know. I'm sure you believe my father did this."

"Gee, I wonder why."

"And I know my mother was cruel to you, so you have no reason to be kind to me, but I… I told them everything I've found out about Dad in the past few years. It doesn't amount to much, but I told them."

Zara knew her anger was aimed at the wrong person. She'd always known that. Easier to act out on when she was sixteen, a bit harder to hold on to these ten years later.

Kate turned on a heel. "Follow me. I'll unlock it for you."

Zara had no choice but to follow Kate into the small building. She glanced back at Jake, close at her heels, tall enough he had to duck to make it through the doors. Kate led them to the back of the building. She unlocked an unmarked door, stepped inside and flipped on a light.

She plunked the keys on the desk in the corner. "Return these to the front office when you're finished with them." Then she swept out of the room.

Well, there was one thing all those big skirts were good for. A dramatic exit.

Zara took a deep breath, studying the tidy desk. Where to begin?

"You failed to mention the old guy your sister ran away with was your best friend's dad," Jake said, and she didn't know what that note in his voice was. Only that it was something more than vaguely interested.

"How do you know she was my best friend?" Zara muttered, flipping through the notebook on Hazeleigh's desk.

"That kind of hurt isn't from a shallow, childhood friendship."

She set the notebook down. "No, I suppose not. But it doesn't matter."

He didn't say anything to that, which made it feel like it *did* matter. But how could it when Amberleigh was dead and Hazeleigh was in jail? And Kate hadn't been her friend for a very long time.

She opened the drawers in Hazeleigh's desk. She

carefully and methodically searched. She read notes, flipped through files. But it was all about that ridiculously fake bank robbery. Nothing that might help Zara figure out why her sister thought she was *safest* in jail.

She moved to the other side, tugging open the much-bigger drawer. She pulled out a cardboard box. Newspaper clippings. Old pictures of the Wilde Bank.

And underneath all that, a wooden box.

She recognized that box. They each had one, hand carved by their great-grandfather. Given to them after he'd passed away. Zara's was in her room, one of the few knick-knacks on her shelf. Sometimes she passed by it and traced the *ZH* and reminded herself who she was and what she came from.

Maybe this was Hazeleigh's, Zara told herself, though she knew Hazeleigh kept hers on her nightstand at the cabin. Zara told herself she'd pick up the box, turn it around and the carved *HZ* would be on the front.

Her vision went a little dim around the corners as she reached out for it. Picked it up, turned it around. The weight and feel of it familiar.

But it's in the wrong place.

There was a Post-it stuck to the front, hiding the engraving that would tell her whose box it was.

She got the sense Jake had stopped looking and was watching what she was doing. Part of her didn't want to do it. Part of her wanted him to. But it was her hand that reached out, that peeled the Post-it away.

And just as she suspected, there was a delicate *AH* carved onto the front.

JAKE THOUGHT ZARA might actually faint. She swayed, but caught herself by grabbing the desk. He put his hand on her back to steady her.

There was something altogether too satisfying in the fact he seemed to be able to do that.

"That's Amberleigh's."

She nodded. "It was one of the few things she took with her."

"Took with her?" Jake asked. His heartbeat picked up a little bit. So they had found something. "You know that for sure?"

"I'm not sure I know anything for sure now. But it was one of her missing belongings. Some clothes. Any money she had. A diary. And this box."

She let out a shaky breath. She held the box like she was afraid to open it, and Jake couldn't blame her there.

"Why wouldn't the police have come to search here?"

She shook her head. "They might still. But Amberleigh was found on our property and plenty to search there. Bloody sweaters and the like."

"Are you going to take it?"

She chewed on her bottom lip, still staring at it. "I guess that depends." With trembling fingers, she lifted the lid. Jake peered over her shoulder.

There were letters inside. The top one was addressed to Hazeleigh. There was no return address.

Zara let out a huff of breath, like in pain. The kind of breath someone expels after a punch. "That's Amberleigh's handwriting."

"You're sure?"

She nodded jerkily. "Postmark is this year." She

began to shake her head, vaguely at first but more insistent with each move. "This can't *be*. If she wrote letters to Hazeleigh, Hazeleigh would have told me. If Amberleigh was back, bringing her box and whatever else, Hazeleigh would have *told* me."

"Should we go to the detective? Show her this?" Jake asked gently.

She didn't stop shaking her head. "I have to know if…"

If it implicated Hazeleigh. Zara didn't want to believe anything bad of her sister, but he understood that if she had to…she'd hide it. She'd protect Hazeleigh, perhaps no matter what she'd done.

Jake didn't know how to feel about that, but he supposed in a way wasn't that what he and his *brothers* were doing? Lying and hiding…for the good of each other.

She didn't open the letter though. She closed the lid. "I need to read these but not here. It's already going to be sketchy enough we came here."

"Come on. Let's return those keys and get back to the ranch. We'll read through them together. Two sets of eyes will get through it quicker." He thought about offering up the rest of the guys, but he had a feeling he knew what Cal would say about all this *involvement*.

There was something else that had him holding back on that front, but he didn't want to contemplate it too much or too hard or remember the way Zara had grinned at a half-naked Landon.

He ground his teeth together and turned on a heel, exiting the building. "Which one's the front office?"

Zara pointed, then started walking for the building

at the center. They walked across the snowy yard in silence. She hid the box inside her jacket, and Jake really didn't know how to feel about the fact more and more things were piling up to implicate Hazeleigh.

But he'd keep an open mind. They'd keep looking for evidence it was someone else. And if Zara had to face facts... Well, he'd help her. With whatever happened.

He looked around the yard. He wasn't sure where the 1800s-dressed woman had gone, but Zara led him to the center building. It was in a little better shape than the two around it. Honestly, they were kind of quaint, but it was the nothingness around the park that surprised him.

Who would build a fort here and why? What were they protecting here in the middle of nothing, with the mountains hovering in the distance? Had this area once drawn more people than it did now?

He stepped into the building after Zara, and suddenly his small, casual interest in history died. Immediately.

There were mannequins...everywhere. They were dressed in old-timey clothes, clearly arranged in scenes to depict life in the fort in the 1800s.

But the mannequins didn't have any *eyes*.

Jake stood struck frozen in place by the grotesque horror of the whole thing. Zara looked back at him, eyes questioning. "What's wrong?"

"Zara, I have faced down entire armies with tanks, grenades and sniper rifles pointed at me, and this is the most terrifying thing I've ever seen."

She turned slowly to face him fully, surprise registering in her expression. "You were in the military." She didn't say it like a question.

Well, he was 0-for-2 in the keeping-things-a-secret category today. And he didn't know what to say to that. There was no denying what he'd said. No easy adoption excuse. And even though the mannequins surrounding them didn't have *eyes*, he still felt like they were watching him.

Judging him.

"You all were in the military," she said with an odd kind of wonder in her voice. "It makes *so* much sense."

"Does it?" he muttered.

"I don't understand why it would be a secret."

"It's a difficult subject, that."

She nodded, as if it had dawned on her. That military included war and people didn't escape that unscathed. Maybe not in the way she might think, but it worked.

He eyed the mannequins warily. "Can we get the hell out of here?"

"I mean, I'm kind of enjoying watching you squirm in terror, but we've got things to do."

He trailed after her as she marched through the scenes of plastic, eyeless horror. "It's not terror," he muttered. But he supposed that's exactly what it was. He suppressed a shudder.

"Hi, Mr. Field," she greeted a small old man in a little room past all the mannequins. He hopped to his feet, hands fluttering about.

"Zaraleigh, oh my goodness. Please tell me this is all a misunderstanding."

Zaraleigh. It had legitimately never occurred to Jake

that, of course, like her *triplet* sisters her name would end in *-leigh*.

The name didn't fit her at all, and it amused him beyond reason. Especially when she looked over her shoulder and glared at him. "Not a word," she muttered. Then she smiled at the old man fussing behind a giant desk piled high with magazines and who knew what all else.

"Hazeleigh didn't do anything wrong," she told the man firmly. "We're working with the detective to make sure she can come home soon. I just had to pick up some of her things. Kate gave me the keys and told me to return them to you." She held them out to him.

"Oh," the old man said. "Well, thank you, dear." He pocketed the keys and smiled blandly up at Zara. *Zaraleigh.* "I'm just so worried about the poor girl, but I suppose you've got everything handled."

"Of course I do," Zara said in a rote tone he'd heard her use a lot. And he realized in the moment that that rote tone wasn't confidence so much as an act.

Because everyone around her seemed to think she had it under control. When this was the kind of situation *no one* would be able to have under control.

"Take care, Mr. Field." She waved at him, then turned and led Jake back out through the museum.

"Zaraleigh," he whispered, to keep himself from thinking about the mannequins and the way their eyeless faces felt as though they were following him.

"I swear to God, Jake, if you ever call me that again, you won't have a tongue to call anyone anything."

"I appreciate the threat, really, but I think we both know you'd have a hard time de-tonguing me."

"All it would take is a sedative slipped into your coffee thermos and patience. Plus a really sharp knife."

He considered the rather detailed fantasy. He gave her a nod. "Impressive."

She made a noise, and her color had come back. She moved with purpose rather than in that shell-shocked way.

"We'll head to the ranch. Read those letters. Go from there." They reached his truck and climbed in. Zara remembered to buckle her own seatbelt this time, and she set the box on her lap, looking at it with trepidation.

He started the truck and backed out of the small parking lot. He began driving toward the ranch.

"Maybe I should read them myself," she said quietly. "That way if something happens, and someone asks you something, you won't know."

He flicked a glance to her briefly. She was staring at the box, tracing the *A* and *H* engraved on the front. She looked lost.

And in desperate need of someone to help her find the way.

"Better to do it quickly and work together to see what we can figure out. If the police start questioning me, I don't have to tell them the truth if it implicates Hazeleigh unfairly."

She looked up at him then. He could feel her gaze, but he kept his on the road. For safety. Not self-preservation.

"If they asked, you'd lie?"

He thought that over. Bit back the words that had popped into his head, unbidden. *If you asked me to.*

"I'd lie about a lot of things, as long as it didn't put anyone in danger."

That was true. It was why he was in Wilde in the first place, wasn't it? Lies to protect the people most important to him.

What was a few more?

For her.

Chapter Ten

Zara wasn't sure what had happened. One minute, she was sitting in Jake's truck, clutching the box in her lap. The next moment, she was blinking her eyes open to a view of the house in front of her. A painful crick in her neck as she sat up straight with a start.

She blinked at the house, then at Jake in the driver's seat. He was playing on his phone, though he set it down when he realized she was awake and alert.

"I...fell asleep?" she asked, because she couldn't quite believe she'd just...dozed off. In the middle of the day. She glanced at the horizon. Well, late afternoon anyway.

"Adrenaline tends to run out, and then the crash."

He'd left the truck running with the heat on. Sat there with her. All the while, a good forty-five minutes had passed since they'd left the fort, and it was only a ten-minute drive from the ranch.

She didn't know what to *do* with him.

"I figure we should read those in my room," he said, nodding to the box that she was still clutching in her lap. "That way we can hide them quickly if we need to."

His room. *Her* room. She was still groggy from the

sleep, and she supposed he was right about a crash. She felt like she'd swum out of some kind of bender. Only instead of alcohol it was worry and stress.

She loosened her grip, flexed her fingers and realized, like her neck, they were cramped and aching. She knew if she went in there with him, with this box and these letters, she was letting him into something…complicated. Potentially dangerous even. Certainly the kind of trouble he and his brothers were hoping to avoid.

"You don't have to sink yourself into this any further. I can handle it on my own." She wanted to believe she could—*had* to. You couldn't *count* on help, even if it was nice to receive once in a while.

She didn't dare look at Jake. Something about telling him she could handle it felt like a lie—even though it wasn't—and she was afraid that would show on her face.

"I'm already in it," he said firmly and got out of the truck before she could say anything else.

Zara blew out a breath that felt all too much like relief. She shouldn't lean on him. She shouldn't depend on anyone's help, but she found herself getting out of the truck and following him into her childhood home.

The rest of the brothers should still be out doing ranch work, if they were following her task list without her around. She assumed they would be, but as the sun set, they'd come home. Maybe Landon had already seen her in Jake's room, and that would be a bit hard to explain, but twice in one day?

"Maybe I should find somewhere else," Zara said, keeping her voice low in case someone *was* home. "I wouldn't want to drag your brothers—"

He put his hand at the small of her back like he was guiding her deeper into the house—when she knew the way. In the dark with her eyes closed.

But that simple touch on her back was…*something*. A prickling heat she didn't know how to classify because that was not…normal.

"I'll handle my brothers," he said. As they reached the staircase, his hand fell away and she could *think* again.

"You'll handle everything?" she asked, climbing the stairs, looking over her shoulder at him following her up.

"No one can handle everything, Zara."

Which felt far more like censure than she knew he meant. She whipped her head around and stared straight ahead, marching perhaps with a little too much purpose to her—his—room.

Her fingers tensed around the box again and she stood in the middle of the room not sure how to proceed. She didn't want to sit on his bed. Where he slept. He'd made it, with a precision that had her remembering what he'd said back at the museum.

Military.

She supposed it might explain some things about the six men. About their secrecy. Their stillness.

She walked over to the window. There was an old chair, small and kind of rickety for a man of his size, situated facing out. Like he sat there and watched the sunset every night.

Just like she'd done every year of her life until the last month.

She looked outside now. Across the land she'd always been so sure she'd tend. Her heart. Her legacy. *Generations* of Harts had built this, and it wasn't hers any longer.

She looked down at the box in her hands. Amberleigh wasn't alive any longer. And it was altogether possible, no matter how impossible it seemed, that Hazeleigh was in some kind of unalterable trouble herself.

Zara needed to get started, but what she really wanted to do was lower herself into the chair and watch the sun slowly sink behind the mountains. The rays of light reaching beyond their craggy peaks, always seemingly *toward* her. Giving her their strength.

She was sitting in the chair before she fully understood it. And once she roused herself from looking at the sinking sun, she glanced at Jake. He stood leaning casually against the door he'd closed behind them. His hands were in his pockets, and though he studied her, it wasn't with the desire for her to get this rolling.

He was so *patient*. Hazeleigh had that kind of patience in her, but in Hazeleigh, it was a certain…separateness. Like she was living in her own world and didn't worry herself with the time in this one.

Zara had no doubt Jake was living in this very world, and that he was just waiting for her to be ready to take the next step.

So she needed to. She looked down at the box, forced herself to open it even though her hands shook. She pulled out the stack of letters and flipped through them, noting names and dates.

"They're all to Hazeleigh from Amberleigh," Zara managed, her voice rustier than she'd like it to be. "They go back to last year."

"Why don't you start at the beginning?" he suggested when she didn't move. Just sat there holding the stack of letters.

Why not? Because she was afraid of what was in them. Afraid of what she would have to do, prove, decide.

Which wasn't acceptable. Fear didn't change the situation in front of you. She should know.

She handed him the top half of the stack, and focused on her own stack rather than how he looked settling himself on his bed.

Where she'd once slept.

She pulled out the letter from the earliest postmarked envelope. The address on the front wasn't the house or the cabin, it was the fort. Hazeleigh had worked there since high school in some capacity, so Amberleigh would have known she could reach her there. Or someone there would know to get the letters to her.

Trying to keep her mind from engaging in the fact her dead sister had folded this paper up, stuck it in the envelope and sent it to her currently jailed sister, and Zara had never been the wiser.

So, she read.

Dear Hazie,
Merry almost-Christmas! Surprised to hear from me? Believe me, I'm surprised to be writing! I could have sent you an email or text I guess, but I knew you'd get a kick out of a handwritten letter. (And people can read emails and texts, can't they? But they'll never know what I wrote you.)
Don't tell Dad. Don't tell Queen Zara. This

is just between you and me, Hazie. I know I can
trust you. And you know we can't trust them.
     When can you get away? I want to see you!
Love,
Amberleigh

Queen Zara. Zara had always hated that nickname.
Yes, she'd been bossier than she needed to be back
then. Okay, always, probably even now, but sometimes
being in charge meant being bossy. Especially when
there was a ranch to run, a father to keep from falling
too far into the bottle, and back then, trying to keep
her grades up and…

She folded the letter back up and put it in the envelope and set it aside. She just had to read through them.
Not defend herself to herself, or to a dead Amberleigh.

Dear Hazie,
I can't meet you until you promise me in writing
that you won't tell Zaraleigh.
Amberleigh

Much shorter that time around. And it didn't mention Dad. Just her. What had Hazeleigh's response said?
How had Hazeleigh gotten a response to Amberleigh?

Zara flipped the envelope back to the front. "The return address on this one is a PO box in Harvey. That's
only about two hours away." Had her sister been that
close all along? Wouldn't that be impossible?

Zara had assumed she'd gotten the heck out of Wyoming, like she'd always wanted to. California or Seattle

or New York City. Anything but craggy mountains and tiny western towns, she'd always said.

Zara had never understood how they were related, let alone shared the same face.

She flipped through the other envelopes, and though sometimes the PO box number changed, Harvey never did.

"All Harvey," Jake confirmed of his stack.

She looked up and he was studying her. "Zara…" He held up the letter he'd been reading. "This last letter…"

Her stomach sank. *Please no.*

"It seems to indicate Hazeleigh was meeting her. Routinely. Up till a month ago."

ZARA SQUEEZED HER eyes shut against what was a clear wave of pain. Jake wished he could take it away for her, but this was bad.

Really bad. The letter clearly spelled out where and when Hazeleigh and Amberleigh would meet. And the fact the letters stopped a month ago, which was probably way too close to when she'd died for comfort.

"She didn't *do* it, Jake."

"I believe you." He knew that looks could be deceiving, and that Hazeleigh's skittishness could have been a con in and of itself. But he also knew Zara, and his own gut instincts.

He also knew Zara *needed* him to believe her, so he simply would.

"I can't give this to the police. Not when they already have evidence against her. This is a nail in the coffin."

"Let's read through the rest of them," Jake said, keeping his voice even, calm. She was both, but he could sense if they didn't keep moving forward she might just shatter. "Maybe it gives some kind of clue. Something we can follow up on. Something that proves Hazeleigh wasn't involved, even if she was meeting Amberleigh."

Zara nodded and immediately pulled out another letter. She flew through them, so he did the same. He'd go over them again, add whatever details he could to the board, but for now they were just skimming for something that cleared Hazeleigh.

He didn't find anything of note. Just places and times to meet. And the recurring assertion Hazeleigh not tell anyone.

"Anything?"

When she didn't answer, he looked up. She had put away all the letters, stacked them again in the neat pile reminding him of Hazeleigh's ruthlessly organized desk. He handed her his stack. She added it to the pile, put them back into the box and closed the lid.

She stared at the box in her lap, still not speaking.

"Zara."

She inhaled deeply. "Nothing except the meetings. They've been meeting for almost a year…"

The "without telling me" was left unsaid but hung in the air just the same.

"I can't tell the police. Not yet. But…"

He waited as she wrestled with the weight of whatever it was she wanted to say.

"I don't know what to do," she finally finished, as if the words had to be pushed out with supreme effort.

Jake didn't either, but that was a pretty consistent place he'd found himself in. He'd learned how to cope and adapt. "Okay. This is what we know. Amberleigh had a PO box in Harvey. Amberleigh and Hazeleigh met at the Fish Inn, whatever *that* is, about once a month for a year." He didn't add the part where the meetings stopped around the same time Amberleigh was likely murdered. Without Hazeleigh saying anything to anyone.

Except for her "feeling" when she'd begged him and Zara not to dig in that spot. It was all too many coincidences not to wonder if Hazeleigh was the murderer, but at the same time, she hadn't really tried to stop him from digging. She'd been in distress, yes, but not physically trying to stop anything.

"Yes, we know all that," Zara agreed. "It's all bad news."

"Maybe." But he couldn't let her live in that bad-news space. "Maybe we just need more information. What if we go to Harvey?"

"Harvey? Like…the Fish Inn?"

"Yeah. We go. We ask around. Maybe someone saw them or overheard something."

"We?"

"Is it ever not going to surprise you that I'm going to work with you on this? We're after the same thing, remember?"

She stared at him for a very long time, her hands still tight around the box. And Jake found himself yet again *unnerved* by the way this woman looked at him, when he'd had foster parents look through him and superiors scream in his face and the enemy so close he could see the whites of his eyes, wishing him *dead*.

It had been easier in a strange way to deal with

those things over the little glimmer of hope he saw in Zara's eyes.

"I'm sorry. I don't really know how not to be surprised by all…this," she said, waving her hand around the room as if to encompass everything. "Not because of you, just because…I'm the one who takes care of things around here. I have since my mother died. Problems with the ranch, struggles with the girls." She stared down at the box. "I thought I did a pretty good job all in all, and Amberleigh is dead and Hazeleigh is in jail."

"And you're working to get justice for both. I can tell you with certainty, Zara, not everybody does that. A lot of people leave you to the wolves, blood or no."

"Well, I'm sorry for that too, then. That you didn't have people who fought for you."

He shrugged, uncomfortable all the ways pieces of himself kept seeming to be uncovered. Unraveled. "I found them eventually." And he had. He'd learned how to stick up for people who needed help.

She stood, still gripping the box tight enough he thought the hinges on the lid might bend and the wood might splinter.

"I have to call the lawyer Thomas told me about."

"Call on the way."

"You want to go now?"

"Why not?"

"Your brothers…"

"There are five of them. They can handle the ranch and live without me for a day or two. And I hate to break it to you, but they're pretty adamant you don't come back to work until after there's a funeral. No matter what happens, you lost your sister. You deserve time off to deal with that."

"You guys are very kind, and I haven't been kind to y—"

"We're military men. We're used to drill sergeants and hard work. You made us feel right at home."

Her mouth almost curved and he was a little too desperate to make it stretch out all the way. "I'm doing this for my brothers and our life here, but I'm also doing it because you're not so bad to have as a friend."

She didn't smile. She almost looked pained.

So he went the opposite route. He grinned at her. "Zaraleigh." He hoped she'd scowl at him or make another de-tonguing threat. But she never quite went to plan, did she?

She moved forward and hugged him. A little bit awkwardly, but it was a friendly, gratitude hug.

Might as well have shot him in the heart.

Chapter Eleven

Zara didn't know what possessed her. Except she didn't have the words to thank him. So she thought a simple hug would do the trick. Better than staring at those blue eyes and getting a little too lost in them.

Or so she'd thought. Turned out hugging a big, tall, hard *man* was not exactly the stuff apologies were made of. And a little more enjoyable than she felt comfortable admitting. She was a strong, independent cowgirl. Why the hell would it feel nice to lean on someone?

She pulled back and fought back a wave of embarrassment. "It's late. We could wait until the morning."

"You don't want to wait. You want answers. I'll grab a few things, some snacks, and then we'll head over to your cabin so you can too. Should we leave the letters here?"

"Let's bring them with."

He nodded.

"I can go get my things on my own. You don't have to…" She wondered if she'd ever be able to stop telling him all the things he didn't *have* to do, that he seemed to want to do or not mind doing.

He turned to look at her, then reached out and put his hand on her shoulder. It seemed to be his main way of giving comfort. His big, *big* hand on her shoulder. "Look, Hazeleigh saying she's safe in jail is a concern. You look exactly like her and the dead person. I'm not sure alone is what you should be right now."

Now he was worried about her *safety*. Oh, she was in so much trouble when this was over and she had some kind of terrible crush on him.

But this wasn't about her feelings, and it certainly wasn't anywhere close to being over. This was about getting Hazeleigh out of jail and figuring out the real murderer. Because someone *had* murdered Amberleigh and buried her on Hart land.

"Okay." What else was there to say? If they drove to Harvey and got some answers…maybe this *could* be over sooner rather than later.

He went to his closet, didn't unlock the part with the board and her bureau that had once hidden her secrets, but he grabbed a beat-up duffel and shoved a few things in it. He disappeared into the hallway to get some things out of the bathroom and then returned. All said and done, he'd packed up in under five minutes.

It was like an out-of-body experience. This couldn't really be her life. Something had happened a month ago. A break with reality. A rip in the fabric of time.

But when he was ready to go, it was her two feet that followed him out of the room and downstairs. Her reality, no matter how unreal it felt.

As they walked into the living room, voices wafted

in from the kitchen area. A lot of low voices, talking and laughing and swearing irritably.

"Just got to pop in and tell them what's up," Jake said, already heading toward the kitchen.

Zara desperately wanted to sneak out the front door rather than face down how to explain all this. But it seemed wrong to duck away. Though she wished she had when five pairs of eyes were staring at her behind Jake with a kind of empathy she didn't understand. It was hard to not feel some guilt over the way she'd viewed them for over a month—as interlopers and enemies.

"We're headed out. Be gone a day or two."

"Day or two," Cal echoed incredulously, frowning at the bag in Jake's hand.

"Yeah, you guys can handle things for a day or two, can't you?"

"Sure. But where on earth are you going?" Cal demanded.

Zara hadn't been any kinder to Cal than she was to Jake or anyone else, but she understood Cal. He was clearly the leader of the group and Jake had just flipped the script. So he had demands. And anger.

"Just got a lead to check out," Jake said, wholly unbothered by the frown on Cal's face.

"Shouldn't you leave that to the police?" Brody offered casually, but there was a pointed look he gave Jake.

Which Jake clearly saw and ignored. "We will if it amounts to anything they can help us with. See you guys later."

He didn't wait around for any more questions or

to assuage all the unsaid concerns very clear on his brothers' faces.

"They don't seem pleased," Zara said in a low voice, but Jake was propelling her into the living room, toward the front door, his hand on the small of her back again.

"They never seem pleased," Jake returned equitably. "Don't worry about it. Let's head over to the cabin."

Zara felt a bit like she was being led around on a leash. Which was a wholly new and strange feeling for her—so much so she didn't know how to fight it. So few people had ever *told* her what to do before, or decided on a course of action *for* her.

There was an odd relief in someone taking the reins.

Her phone rang as they approached the cabin and she pulled it out. Wincing a little bit at the readout on her screen. "Hey, Dad."

"Z-sara."

He'd been drinking. She squeezed her eyes shut. "You okay?"

He swore at her, a filthy stream of words. She'd opened her mouth to cut them off, but the phone was plucked out of her hand before she could. Jake marched in front of her, presumably clicked End on the call and then dropped the phone into his coat pocket.

"No need for that," Jake said firmly, his jaw tight. He gestured to her door as a sign to have her unlock it.

Zara tried to process it all. She should probably be angry with him. He had no right to hang up on her father *for* her, or pocket her phone, or tell her what to do, or *help* her with this whole damn thing.

But no matter how she tried to stir up her own usual

anger, she just thought…he'd defended her in a strange way. Protected her from having to deal with her father when he was acting like that.

But she did have to deal with it. "I should go check on him."

Jake eyed her, arms crossed over his chest almost casually. But there was a tension there. "Has interceding when he's drunk ever gone well for you?"

She supposed it shouldn't surprise her that Jake would see through the situation so easily. He seemed to see through everything, understand all sorts of things she'd never verbalized. And his question had her wilting, because no, she'd never been able to solve her father's issues. Least of all when he was drinking. "No."

"If you're worried about his welfare, call the cops. But don't put yourself in a position like that."

"Let me guess. You have experience with that too."

He laughed, but there was a bitterness in it she hadn't heard from him before. "When it comes to the foibles of humans, there isn't a lot I haven't dealt with."

"I suppose you swoop in on your white horse every time?"

He studied her for a long while, something in his eyes as foreign to her as being led. "Not every time," he said with a gravity that made her heart beat just a little too fast.

She swallowed and fumbled with her keys, not meeting his gaze anymore. She really needed to stop that. Keep her wits about her—impossible when his eyes met hers. She jammed the key into the lock, but his hand came over hers before she twisted it.

"Wait," he ordered. "Something isn't right."

JAKE SUPPOSED, IN a way, it was like Hazeleigh's "feelings" as Zara had described them. He couldn't explain to her what was wrong, only that he had a sudden sensation that something was off.

There was a...smell in the air that didn't belong. An odd stillness to the air that should have been bustling with bird flight and breezes dancing through the...

Sand and desert and the bone-deep terror that nothing was going as it should. The faint sound of gunfire, the arid air making his eyes gritty and yet he couldn't blink. If he blinked...

"Jake?"

He started at Zara's voice, the current moment sliding back into focus. Her hand rested on his chest, and there was genuine concern all over her face.

He hadn't had a moment like that in a while. They'd been debriefed enough to know that certain...residual physical responses were normal. Nightmares, shakes, flashbacks. As long as they didn't interfere with his daily life, it was simply a...side effect, so to speak, of his military career.

They were rare, and he was rational, so he wasn't going to freak out about it.

But that didn't mean he was thrilled it had happened in front of Zara.

He cleared his throat. "Sorry."

Her hand fell off his chest, and he had the urge to grab it. Hold on to it. He didn't. He looked at the cabin critically. There wasn't anything off that he could see. But he didn't know the cabin as well as she did. "Does anything look out of place? Anything at all. Not just big things. Small, inconsequential things too."

She turned slowly, her concerned gaze changing to one of speculation as she studied her house. She turned in a slow circle, looking up and then down. She frowned at the pot of flowers on the porch. "It's been moved."

"Moved?"

She pointed at the depression of snow that made it clear the pot had moved an inch or two to the left. "Not by much. An animal searching for scraps could have done it. I could have done it, but it's definitely been moved and…"

"And?"

"I keep a spare key under that pot. We don't use it very often, because we don't lock up very often, but we keep it there when we do have to lock up. Which I have been, obviously."

"Does anyone know besides Hazeleigh?"

"I doubt it. Dad, maybe? But he doesn't come out here very often. He did come out the other day, but I really don't think he knew it was there. And if he's been…"

She didn't say it, but she didn't have to. He'd heard the muffled drunken tirade. The lack of surprise on Zara's face. A kind of exhausted acceptance as the color leached out of her face.

Yeah, he didn't have very many memories before the foster home, but that was one of them. He'd been too little to do anything about it then, so he'd be damned if he stood around and let it happen to someone now.

"Stay out here," he told Zara, putting his bag on the little rocking chair they had on the porch and digging around until he found his gun case. He unzipped it and pulled the revolver out. With quick efficient movements, keeping his body between the weapon and Zara's view of it, he loaded it. "I'll go in and make sure no one's in there."

"But why would anyone be in there? Why would *I* be in danger?"

He didn't know the answer to that. He only knew it was better to be safe than sorry. "I'm just going to check it out. Stay put. That's all you have to do." He pulled her phone out of his pocket and handed it to her.

Just in case.

She eyed the gun warily, but she didn't say anything as she took her phone. She pulled her keys out of her pocket and unlocked the door. He touched her arm with his free hand before she could turn the knob and open it.

"Just wait here," he said firmly, hoping she would listen. A few days ago, he knew she wouldn't have. She had been sure of her place in her little world and confident it was her role to march through it in charge.

Then they'd found Amberleigh buried in the ground.

He had never met Amberleigh, but even for him, it was a turning point. All of Cal's carefully instituted rules about boundaries and space had gone out the window. And Jake was too used to turning points not to go with the flow.

He moved into the cabin and did a sweep, mostly looking for evidence of someone or anything dangerous. He didn't see anything as he went through each room, every closet and possible hiding spot. He retraced his steps, checking a second time until he was satisfied the cabin was clear.

He returned to the porch and gestured for her to come in. "It's clear, but I want you to look around and see if you notice anything I didn't."

He followed her as she walked through the cabin. He'd always thought she'd had a bit of a poker face, but today, she seemed to have lost the ability. Every emotion chased over her features. Worry, concern, self-doubt. He could practically hear her inner thoughts. *Was that chair really here? Or was it angled the other way?*

"Nothing's been moved," she said, hesitating in front of Hazeleigh's room. "But…" She trailed off and then inched forward, like she had to force herself to make the move.

Jake followed close behind, noticing that Hazeleigh's room was ruthlessly organized but still cozy and feminine, unlike Zara's room, which had been…utilitarian at best. And not particularly organized. It would definitely be easier to see if someone had messed with Hazeleigh's things.

She walked over to the nightstand next to Hazeleigh's bed. There was a box just like the one that had been in Hazeleigh's desk at the fort.

"It's backwards," Zara said, swallowing. "The initials should be facing the bed, but they're facing the wall. Like the pot, it could just be coincidence. The police searched her room after all."

But she reached forward and, with obvious trepidation, lifted the lid. Then she lifted the whole box and gave it a little shake. She turned it over and pushed something so the bottom popped open.

She peered in, then jumped back, the box falling onto the bed. She whirled to face him, her eyes squeezed shut.

"What is it?" Jake demanded, striding forward and looking into the box's false bottom himself. For supposedly innocent people, there were sure a lot of intricate hiding places.

There was a necklace in the bottom. With what looked like blood crusted in the chain.

"It was Amberleigh's," Zara whispered. "She…" She cleared her throat. "She came home with it one day. She never told anyone if she bought it or if someone gave it to her. But after she disappeared with Mr. Phillips, we always assumed…"

"We could call the police," Jake said carefully. "Maybe they would believe that someone had planted it. This Mr. Phillips…"

Zara eyed him. "I don't think I can deal in maybes. Not with Hazeleigh in jail and that being hidden in the false bottom the police wouldn't have originally searched."

He nodded. "Then we'll take it with us."

She nodded faintly, looking around Hazeleigh's room. "I think someone put this in here today, Jake. But that pot could have been moved by a million different things. This box could have been backwards for days. Maybe it's paranoia…"

"No, I agree with you. Something didn't feel right out there. I don't think we missed whoever put this here by very long."

"They expect the police to come search again. They must."

Jake nodded. "So let's get out of here. And do a little searching of our own."

FREE BOOKS GIVEAWAY

2 FREE SUSPENSE BOOKS!

2 FREE SUSPENSEFUL ROMANCE BOOKS!

GET UP TO FOUR FREE BOOKS & TWO FREE GIFTS WORTH OVER $20!

We pay for everything!

See Details Inside

Complete the survey below and return it today to receive up to 4 FREE BOOKS and FREE GIFTS guaranteed!

FREE BOOKS GIVEAWAY
Reader Survey

1	2	3
Do you prefer stories with suspensful storylines?	Do you share your favorite books with friends?	Do you often choose to read instead of watching TV?
○ YES ○ NO	○ YES ○ NO	○ YES ○ NO

YES! Please send me my Free Rewards, consisting of **2 Free Books from each series I select** and **Free Mystery Gifts**. I understand that I am under no obligation to buy anything, no purchase necessary see terms and conditions for details.

❑ **Harlequin® Romantic Suspense** (240/340 HDL GRRU)
❑ **Harlequin Intrigue® Larger-Print** (199/399 HDL GRRU)
❑ **Try Both** (240/340 & 199/399 HDL GRR6)

FIRST NAME   LAST NAME

ADDRESS

APT.#   CITY

STATE/PROV.   ZIP/POSTAL CODE

EMAIL ❑ Please check this box if you would like to receive newsletters and promotional emails from Harlequin Enterprises ULC and its affiliates. You can unsubscribe anytime.

HI/HRS-122-FBG22

HARLEQUIN® Reader Service **—Terms and Conditions:**

Chapter Twelve

Zara grabbed a few things. Mostly things that no one would miss. She packed a travel toothbrush, a pair of jeans and a long-sleeved tee and flannel that wouldn't be missed out of the other pairs she had that all looked the same.

She mussed up her bed a little bit, so anyone would assume she'd slept in it, even though she didn't plan to tonight.

Because if someone put that bloody necklace in Hazeleigh's box, they expected the police to come back again.

She put said box, bloody necklace and all, in her bag.

Part of her felt like she was making a mistake. She should take it to the police and trust them. Thomas was a good police officer. Laurel seemed like an empathetic detective, and Zara knew Thomas looked up to the woman as a kind of mentor, which meant she had to be good at her job.

Zara should trust what she'd always been brought up to trust, but as she stepped into the living room, Jake was there. He still held the gun, though relaxed at his side rather than with that flinty-eyed stare he'd had when he'd pulled it out of his bag in the first place.

He stood there, tall and strong, looking through the window to the dark world outside.

She trusted him. More than her cousin. More than the detective. More than just about anyone.

She didn't know why. She couldn't begin to explain it. Maybe it was something about the way he'd held that gun, or held her when she cried, or just kept offering to help.

She knew he'd had some sort of…flashback out there. His eyes had gone unfocused, his breathing had increased, and she'd just known he wasn't there with her. He was reliving something else.

Her heart had broken for him. And when she'd said his name, he'd come back.

She supposed it didn't mean anything. She didn't know anything about the military or what kind of scars it might leave with a person. How anyone dealt with them or how a soldier brought themselves back to the current world when lost in an old, painful one.

But she'd reached out and touched him, and he'd gotten to work. Protecting her. She wanted to make it about keeping his brothers out of trouble. She knew she should.

But it felt so much more personal than that the longer this went on, the more he was essentially lying for her.

"Ready?" he asked, without turning around. He'd sensed her or heard her and knew she was staring at him. She wondered how he did that, how Hazeleigh listened to "feelings." How anyone saw or sensed any more than the here and now.

But then she thought about the way she knew a calf would come or when the leaves would burst forth in spring. When she could smell rain or snow in the air. Because her life was attune to the ranch, to her world. It was the same, all in all.

"Yes, I'm ready." Because she didn't know what was going on, but she knew her sister wasn't a murderer. And whoever *was* had spent some time framing Hazeleigh for it.

She'd made a promise to her mother, not that Mom had asked, that she'd protect her sisters. She couldn't protect them from Mom dying, but she could look out for them. Be a stand-in mother to them.

She had failed Amberleigh. She couldn't fail Hazeleigh too.

They walked out to Jake's truck and climbed in. The sunset had completely faded and stars winked above. They followed the moon out to the highway.

Jake didn't ask for directions. He just drove. A country station offered jovial drinking songs at low tones.

They said nothing for a very long time. She had forgotten to pay attention to the time, and instead counted the stars like she used to do when she'd been too worried to sleep.

"Someone's following us," Jake said quietly.

She started to whip her head around, but he let out a sharp "don't" and she stopped. Looking at him instead.

"We don't want them to know we know they're following us," he said. His voice was certain, his grip on the steering wheel still casual. His gaze flicked to the rearview mirror. "Do you know anyone who drives a silver or gray Ford pickup?"

"I know a hundred people who drive that, Jake."

"Okay. Any cops?"

She thought about Thomas and the other cops she knew. "Not that I know of, but it's a pretty common vehicle around Wilde. Maybe it's a coincidence."

"Maybe," he agreed.

She didn't believe his agreement for a second.

She slowly moved her face to look forward again. Then she looked in the rearview mirror. She saw a pair of headlights and maybe the slight glimmer that offered the color of the truck, but mostly his eyesight must have been much better than hers.

"So, what do we do?"

He didn't say anything at first. He was thinking it through, weighing options.

Because he didn't know what to do any more than she did.

"We shouldn't go to the Fish Inn if we're really being followed."

"Right, but we need to go somewhere convincing. If they're following, just following, they want to know where we're going," Jake said, mulling it over. "Somewhere two people might randomly drive to on a Wednesday night in December."

"We're going to pass through Bent in a little bit. There's not much there, but there is a saloon."

"A saloon," Jake said with the ghost of a smile. "You all take your Wild West very seriously."

It might have been a little funnier if they weren't being followed. But she still smiled. "Oh, you have no idea."

JAKE FOLLOWED ZARA's directions off the highway to the tiny town of Bent. Much like Wilde, there wasn't much to the town. A Main Street with a few of the basics, and at the end of that Main Street a…yes, saloon.

It looked like every saloon in every Western movie or TV show he'd ever seen. Wood siding and a walkway in front of it, a ramshackle overhang, hand-painted signs he couldn't quite make out in the dark and the odd glow of the neon signs—the only thing not very western about it.

Except one—a neon, centaur-like creature, half horse, half very busty woman, a blinking sack of gold hanging off her saddle. And the name of the bar in bright lights: Rightful Claim.

Jake pulled his truck to a park in the small gravel lot on the far side of the building. For a small town and a weekday night, there was a pretty full lot. They got out of the truck, and Jake watched the road for their followers.

"We'll go in and order a drink," Jake said, letting Zara lead the way to the front door. "After we order, you'll stay put inside and I'm going to come out and take a look around."

"Is that safe?" Zara asked, her footsteps echoing on the wood-planked walkway.

Jake didn't tell her he had his gun in his coat pocket. "I'll be careful."

She walked up to the entrance of the bar. They were actual swinging saloon doors. Jake followed Zara inside, watching as the pickup truck that had been following them drove down Main Street past the entrance.

Jake tried to get a glimpse of the driver without being too obvious, but it was too dark.

Inside, rough-hewn wood planks made up the walls of the main area, high-top tables littered the room. Lining the doorway were pictures of the place over the years, a few photos including a signed one of country singer Daisy Delaney.

In the back was a long bar. Most of the stools pulled up to it were taken by men in heavy work coats. Two men tended said bar, both tattooed and bearded, laughing with each other and the patrons.

Jake put his hand at the small of Zara's back, propelling her forward. Her footsteps slowed, practically pushing back against his hand. "Uh, Jake. There's something I kind of forgot about when I suggested Bent and the saloon."

"Oh, yeah, what's that?" he asked, only half paying attention as he kept an eye behind them at the door, just in case the people or person following them was bold enough to follow them right into the bar.

"You know the detective? Laurel Delaney-Carson?"

"Yeah."

"One of those bartenders might be her husband. He owns the place."

Jake's head snapped forward again, taking in the two men behind the bar serving drinks. *Hell.* "Yeah, that might have been helpful information before we came inside." Still he didn't stop their forward movement. Best not to draw any attention. "Does he know who you are?"

"I don't know. It's possible. Thomas is good friends

with their family, but I've never met them in a formal introduction way."

But if the detective brought any of her work home, it was possible the husband knew about the triplets who were his friend's cousins. One dead, one in jail and one right here.

"Stay behind me," Jake said quietly. "I'll order for both of us. Just try to look casual, but keep your head out of the bartenders' lines of vision as much as possible."

Zara nodded and fell back behind him a little bit as they finally approached the bar. Jake squeezed into a spot between taken stools, leaning his elbow on the bar and smiling at the bartender. "Can I get two beers? Whatever you've got in a bottle."

He didn't look back at Zara to make sure she was listening to him. That might bring attention to her too.

He fished a twenty out of his pocket and slid it across the bar as the bartender put two bottles out for him. He waited for the change, outwardly the most patient man alive. Inwardly, strung tighter than a drum.

He thought the bartender gave him a speculative, careful look, but Jake wasn't sure if it was simply because he was a new face in what was surely a small-town bar that didn't get many new faces, or because he recognized…something.

He pocketed the change, took the beers and then turned and gave Zara a little nudge. "Anywhere to sit?" he asked brightly.

"Yeah, looks like that table in the corner is free," she returned, and he was impressed with how casual she sounded. Her body was tense, but someone would have to be looking for that reaction to see it.

He hoped.

The table in the back hadn't been cleared since the previous guests had left, but they both took it anyway. Jake made sure Zara took the seat that kept her back to the bar.

She blew out a relieved breath when they sat down, but they were hardly out of hot water. He had to focus on the biggest threat at the moment—which wasn't the detective's husband figuring them out. It was who was following them. And why.

"I'm going to pretend to get a phone call and go outside. All you have to do is stay put and try to remain inconspicuous. I'll make sure the truck didn't stop around here to follow us any farther."

"What if they did stop around here to follow us farther?"

"Then we'll know, and I'll come back in and we'll decide what to do next. Okay?"

She was frowning, but she nodded, clutching the bottle of beer in front of her. "Okay."

He gave it another minute, then pulled his phone out of his pocket and pantomimed telling Zara he'd be back in a minute before he stood and weaved his way out of the bar. He didn't look back at the bartenders, no matter how much he wanted to. Didn't look back at Zara for a whole host of reasons he didn't want to identify.

He stepped outside, pretended to talk on his phone, all the while studying the dark world around him. The lights of the saloon were about the only ones on in all of Main Street. A building a ways down had some kind of security light on, but that was about it.

He walked toward the parking lot, still pretending to talk on his phone. He went to his truck, looking at every other one in the parking lot. A lot of them looked like the truck that had been following him, but if he touched the hood, they were cold and no one was in them.

He reached into his own truck, pretended to get something from the glove compartment, then made his way back to the saloon. Instead of heading toward the front though, he decided to make a quick walk around back to see if there was any more parking or an alley someone might have driven down.

He kept to the shadows. He tried to listen, but the voices and music from inside the bar wafted outside and it was hard to tell if the engine he heard was coming from behind the building or out on Main Street.

He slid his gun out of his pocket but kept it close to his side. In the back, there was a car idling. A silver Ford pickup.

Jake kept his back to the wall of the building and inched closer and closer, trying to get *some* glimpse of the man sitting in the driver's seat. He noted the license plate, committed the letters and numbers to memory. He couldn't make out any driver though.

Which put a little bit of a wrinkle into his plan.

So he'd have to come up with a new one.

Chapter Thirteen

Zara felt like every muscle in her body was tensed against her will. She kept her gaze trained straight ahead. Hung on the wall was a painting of a woman on a horse, leaning over and embracing a cowboy who was holding a bouquet of flowers behind his back.

It was a surprisingly sweet painting compared to some of the more rustic or bawdy decor. And if she thought about that, she could almost forget what Jake was outside doing.

Putting himself in danger. For her.

For himself and his brothers.

You really think so?

On and on, in circles. So she traced the flowers with her eyes, the purples and pinks. He was hiding them behind his leg. Would he give them to the woman? What would her reaction be? Why did he look a little too like Jake in her imagination, when the painting didn't look a thing like him?

Zara jumped a foot when someone behind her said her name. Her full name.

"Zaraleigh Hart."

The woman's voice was unfamiliar, and Zara was

about to turn, but something sharp was being jammed into her back, *through* her coat, and she went immediately still.

The woman leaned over her, standing behind her and likely hiding her from view of anyone around them. Her voice was low in Zara's ear. "You're going to stand. Slowly. Then you're going to head to the back and calmly follow signs to the women's bathroom."

Zara was terrified, but even shaken with fear, she didn't take well to orders. "If I don't?"

"Your friend outside won't know what hit him."

Zara's entire body went cold. "What do you mean?"

"Stand. Go to the bathroom."

Zara considered her options. She knew how to fight, but the woman clearly had a knife of some kind. Zara could stand up and yell and hopefully *someone* would help her.

But what about Jake? Outside, all alone? He wouldn't know what hit him. She couldn't... No, she couldn't let that happen.

She stood.

"Don't look back at me. Just turn and walk to the bathroom."

She did what the woman said, though she tried to see the woman out of her peripheral vision. But that sharp object jammed into her back again, and Zara stepped forward, weaving her way through the tables and people as the woman followed her, knife concealed by the woman's sleeve but definitely the sharp end breaking through the skin of Zara's back.

Zara glanced at the two men behind the bar as she passed. They were chatting and serving drinks, but as if he sensed he was being stared at, the one who'd served Jake looked up. The one she thought she recognized from the detective's phone.

She didn't look away. She didn't do anything. She just held his gaze, stared at him, *willing* him to see that something wasn't quite right.

He frowned vaguely, but someone must have called his name because he looked back to one of the patrons and smiled.

Zara weighed her options as she went into a little hallway that led to a back room. There was a men's bathroom, a women's bathroom and a swinging door she assumed went into a kitchen or storage room. There was also a little staircase that must have gone up to an apartment of some kind.

There weren't any people at the moment, but surely someone would come to go to the bathroom or emerge from those kitchen doors.

"See that door at the end of the hall? You're going to walk right out it. There's a truck waiting for you."

Zara studied the exit that likely led out behind the building. A truck waiting for her? That was not ideal. "And what about my friend?"

Out of the corner of her eye, Zara saw the woman *smirk*.

Which solved *that* for Zara. She knew how to fight. She'd learned in middle school the quickest way to get a boy to leave her or her sisters alone was to break his nose. If they were afraid of her, they didn't mess with Hazeleigh and Amberleigh so much.

This woman had a knife, but she wasn't much taller than Zara. It was hard to tell with all the loose-fitting black clothing she was wearing, but Zara thought she had the weight advantage on her.

She took a deep breath, remembered to keep her body loose so the woman wouldn't anticipate the blow, and then jerked her elbow up. She didn't get a full elbow to the chin before the woman jumped back, but between that and the glancing blow, she had enough space she could jump out of the knife's reach and whirl to face the woman.

She raised her fists, ready to fight her way out of this. The woman stood there with a sneer, holding the knife in one hand.

"You're going to regret that."

"You're going to regret trying to kidnap me." God, she hoped *that* was true. She eyed the entrance to the main part of the bar behind the woman. It was her best shot, because while she could run out the back door, she'd likely be running either into the dark or the truck the woman mentioned was waiting to take her away.

"What the hell do you want with me?"

"It's a shame you can't ask your sister." The woman flashed a nasty smile and then started advancing on Zara, knife pointed as if ready to do some damage.

Zara assumed the woman was referring to Amberleigh when she mentioned "sister," but what did she know? Maybe Hazeleigh was mixed up in *this* too.

Whatever this was.

Zara backed up, but knew she only had a few steps. If she kept backing up, she'd back right out the door and into whoever was waiting's hands.

She'd never fought with anyone wielding a knife, and she realized that while she'd never minded the threat of getting punched in the face, getting stabbed was a little more concerning.

"Things are going to go a lot better for you if you just follow orders."

Zara laughed. "I'm not stupid. Whatever you want from me is not *better* for me than getting far away from you."

"Suit yourself. We can fight. I'll win." She twirled the knife. "I do have this and all. But for taking up my valuable time…" She pulled a phone out of her pocket. "All it takes is one phone call to end your friend."

Zara kept her fists bunched and in front of her, but she eyed the phone. The woman could be lying, and Jake had been in the military. Maybe he could handle himself. He was out there looking for whoever had followed them.

Maybe she should trust him to take care of himself.

Put herself first. Get herself out of this. Then worry about all the rest, because this woman had a knife, and a phone that could apparently, possibly end Jake's life.

No, she really couldn't take a chance on that. Surely she could survive being stabbed. It wasn't a gunshot after all. Even that was *survivable*, wasn't it? She'd been kicked by horses and cows and even a donkey once when she'd been very small and still learning the ins and outs of ranching with very little guidance from her father.

She wasn't a little girl anymore. So, she charged. Apparently it was surprising enough the woman *didn't* think to jab the knife into her stomach. The woman fell backward, the phone falling out of her hand.

Sadly, the knife didn't go with quite such ease, even

as Zara landed on top of the woman. The woman reared back as if to use it, but Zara grabbed her arm and wrestled it away from her body. They tussled like that, Zara feeling a bit like she was in a calf-roping competition.

If only she had some rope.

She managed to put all her body weight on the arm holding the knife, but the woman rolled over with enough force Zara rolled across the floor, and the woman now had her arm free to stab.

They jumped to their feet at the same time. This time Zara was facing the exit, with the woman in front of her. Zara could easily bolt back into the bar.

She took a step back.

"I'm going to take real pleasure in hurting him," the woman said. "And you, eventually."

"If he doesn't hurt you first," Zara replied, hoping to God it was possible Jake could handle himself. Surely if *she* could, *he* would.

She took another step back, toward the bar and people and *help*.

What about that bloody necklace?

Help was just as dangerous as the woman with the knife, but one option she had a better chance of talking her way out of. Maybe. She took another step back and into a wall—

Or what she thought was a wall. When she looked over her shoulder, she saw nothing but a man's broad chest. She looked up and realized it was one of the bartenders. He had his arms crossed over his chest and was eyeing the woman with the knife. "I called the cops."

The woman flicked a glance at the exit behind her, then made a run for it. Zara turned to face him.

The bartender studied her with concern. "You okay? Should I run after her?"

Zara couldn't look at him and his kind concern. The woman had run—without a phone now but she still had a knife. And she might be going after Jake. Jake was still out there.

"I have to go," Zara heard herself say, stepping away from the man. She started backing away, toward the exit where the woman had gone.

"You're one of Hart's cousins, aren't you?" The bartender held up his hands in a peace gesture as he moved toward her for every step she took back. "Laurel Delaney-Carson is my wife. She's working on a case for you, right? Why don't you come on upstairs? You can wait for the cops to get here. I called Thomas specifically. He lives just down the road, he should be here any minute."

Zara knew he was being kind. That he'd attempted to help her by calling Thomas. "I can't." She edged more and more for the door. She had to find Jake. They had to get out of here.

Maybe the woman with the knife was a problem, but so was the bloody necklace in her bag in Jake's truck. It pointed at too many things that made Hazeleigh guilty, and Jake guilty by association.

Zara made it to the door, pushed it open.

"They're just going to come after you. Those guys. The police." He said this sympathetically.

Zara nodded. He was probably right. But she couldn't let that stop her. "That phone on the floor was the woman's. Make sure the police know that. And could you tell Thomas not to follow us? I know he won't listen, but maybe if he understood I had to do this. That I'm not just… I *had* to do it. Tell him that."

"If you're scared, we can protect you here. You're among friends here. Hart is my daughter's godfather. I promise—"

She believed him. But that didn't change her reality. "I have to go." And she bolted.

Jake heard the footsteps, too close and out of place with where he was crouched in the shadows. He had a mere second to whirl and react.

He blocked an arm that slashed down at him, holding a knife. He punched with the other arm, but the guy was big and muscled and mean, and the blow didn't seem to affect him.

The man stood facing him, a knife glinting in the faint glimmer of a streetlight a ways down the alley.

Jake adjusted the gun in his hand, lifted and aimed. "Looks like you brought a knife to a gunfight, friend."

"Quieter though," the man said, his nasty smile glinting in the sweep of far-off headlights. "You fire that gun at me you're going to have to answer a lot of questions from the cops."

The man was right, of course, but Jake had to pretend like that didn't matter to him. He shrugged. "I think I'll come out all right."

"You'd be surprised." The man laughed, edging closer, the knife still gripped and held out like it could trump a gun. "You don't know what you're dealing with."

Which was true. Clearly. This was getting more

complicated by the minute. It made Jake even more leery of shooting. Made this all the more…precarious.

Someone clattered out of the back entrance of the bar. "Leave him," a woman said, running for the idling truck. "Cops are on the way," the woman said on a hiss. "We'll come back for her later."

The man was momentarily distracted, and Jake could have shot him. Not to kill, just to wound, but the man wasn't wrong. It would bring up far, far too many questions and the kind of attention he and Zara couldn't afford.

So he charged instead. He could use the gun as a different weapon. Knock him down, get a good blow in. But the man held fast, going with the momentum rather than letting it knock him off his feet.

And the knife easily slashed down, into Jake's arm with a screaming bolt of pain.

Jake didn't react, kept the groan of pain deep within, didn't jerk away, though it was a hard-won fight with his body's reflexes. He did dodge the second swipe, then managed a decent blow against the guy's chin with the butt of the gun.

But the woman was screaming at the guy, and he retreated, running to the truck. Leaving Jake…dazed and struggling to tell his body to move. To chase.

He couldn't take them both unless he was willing to shoot, and he couldn't leave Zara behind. But surely he couldn't let them run. He couldn't…

The truck peeled out of the lot, sirens beginning to sound dimly. Another shadowy figure stumbled out of the back exit, but this time he knew it was Zara.

"We have to go," she said. "The cops are coming."

She grabbed his arm and began pulling him in the opposite direction his assailant had gone. Each step was a jarring pain, but he simply accepted it. Like he'd always been taught to do.

She took his arm, stopping him as the streetlight revealed where the knife had slashed through his coat, shirt and arm. "Jake."

The horror in her voice was…strange. He didn't understand it. This was hardly the worst injury he'd suffered. He felt the gritty sand in his eyes, heard the distant echo of gunfire. Of explosions.

He blinked. *Not here. Not now.*

"I'm okay," he said through gritted teeth. It hurt. Damn it all to hell, it hurt. But he'd live. He began to pull her toward the truck this time. *Here. Now.* "Let's get out of here."

"You're hurt. You need a hospital." She stopped at the truck, looking up and down the road. "Maybe we should just tell the truth. Maybe…"

"Is that what you want to do, Zara?" he asked harshly.

She looked up at him with a pain in her eyes that twisted his gut. "I wish it was."

"Come on." He opened the driver's side door, but she snagged the keys as he pulled them from his pocket.

"I'm driving." And she hopped into the driver's seat.

Chapter Fourteen

Zara drove out of Bent, headlights off, slow and in the opposite direction the sirens had come from. When no lights flashed behind them for a good thirty minutes, Zara assumed the police had gone after their attackers for the time being, but they'd circle back to her and Jake soon enough.

She supposed it was the adrenaline wearing off when she began to shake. Still, she gripped the steering wheel as hard as she could and snuck a look at Jake.

With quick, efficient movements, he'd wrapped a bandana from the glove compartment around the horrible gash in his arm. Now he sat very still and said nothing as she drove toward the Fish Inn. It was their destination. That couldn't change.

He seemed unaffected, and yet she knew he was affected. There was something off about him. He wasn't *sharp*. Everything he did was careful and studied, but not *easy*.

And he didn't offer a plan. A course of action. He said nothing at all, which wasn't like him and might have scared her if she was a lesser woman. But she was a woman used to taking charge.

"We'll stick with the plan, but we'll get a room," Zara decided. Jake had been calling the shots, but he was hurt, and this was *her* deal. Amberleigh's bloody necklace. Hazeleigh in jail. *She* was the one in charge of keeping her sisters safe.

Not so great at your job these days, are you?

It seemed unfair the words would sound like her father's voice, when he'd never care enough to pass judgment on her lack of success.

"We'll need to clean you up and get some bandages." If that would work. Jake's wound looked like the kind of cut that needed stitches. "Maybe there's a doctor in town that could—"

"A bandage will do," he said with the same gritted teeth determination that made her wonder just what he'd seen in that military service of his. What he was seeing now. Back at her porch, he'd had some sort of flashback, if she had to guess. Was this the same?

He didn't offer that information up, and she didn't ask. She focused on driving. She focused on one foot in front of the other. It was the only way to get through anything.

When the sign for the Fish Inn came into view, Zara felt a relief she knew was disproportionate. They were hardly out of the woods, but she didn't think she could concentrate on what she needed to—Hazeleigh and the necklace and the framing—until Jake was…okay.

She drove around the parking lot, looking for the most out-of-the-way darkened spot. She didn't know if the cops would catch on enough to look for Jake's truck, way out here, but they had to be careful.

She parked in the back, in a darkened corner. They

both got out of the truck and collected their bags before meeting at the front of the truck. She grabbed her hat and pulled it low on her head. She grabbed a hat from the back she assumed was his and handed it to him.

He settled it on his head, pulling his low like she had. In the dim light, he looked like a dangerous cowboy. Which should have been amusing since she'd been the one to teach him to ride a horse.

She didn't feel *amused*.

"Keys," Jake ordered. There was a strange note to his voice. A distance she didn't understand and didn't know how to parse. She frowned at him, but it was his truck, so she handed them over. She adjusted her bag on her shoulder. "Maybe I should carry your bag."

"It's a flesh wound on one arm. I'll survive," he said and began walking toward the hotel entrance.

Zara had to scurry to catch up to his certain, long-legged pace. When they stepped through the automatic doors, he slid his arm—his hurt arm—around her shoulders and smiled at the young woman behind the counter as they approached. "I don't suppose you have a room available. The wife and I didn't get nearly as far on our drive as we wanted to, and this is the first place I've seen to stay in miles."

The wife. Zara knew he was acting, but *wife* and *room* meant they'd be in the *same* room tonight and that wasn't exactly what she'd had in mind. Though she wasn't sure *what* she'd had in mind.

"We have a few rooms open," the woman said, typing something into her computer. "Just one night?"

"That should do it."

"I'll just need an ID and a credit card." Jake moved

to pull his wallet out of his pocket, and she noticed the slight wince that he tried to hide behind the hat and his own stoic…whatever.

Zara turned her attention to the woman at the computer. "Do you have a first aid kit I could borrow? My *husband* here took a little tumble and needs some patching up."

The receptionist eyed Jake dubiously, and he smiled, a little glassy-eyed, as he handed the cards to her. "Clumsy me."

The woman took the cards, moved around copying the license and running the card. She handed both back to Jake, including key cards with the room number written on the envelope they were inside of. She grabbed a small white box from underneath the counter and slid it to Zara.

"Thanks. Is it okay if I bring it back in the morning?"

"Sure. Your bill will be under the door in the morning too. Checkout by eleven."

"Thanks."

They turned and walked toward the elevator. Jake stumbled a little, and Zara's heart lurched as she reached out to steady him. Was he really that bad off?

He slumped against the wall until the elevator doors opened and they stepped inside. She opened her mouth to demand what was the matter, but he… He was himself again. Standing straight. Completely fine.

It hit her then. He'd been pretending to be drunk.

Well, it wasn't exactly inconspicuous, but hopefully it made the tumble and first aid kit seem a little less sketchy.

They walked to their room in utter silence, and Jake unlocked the door and held it open for her. She stepped inside the run-of-the-mill-if-a-little-dingy hotel room.

With one bed.

She stared at it for a moment too long. Silly to worry about *sleep* when there were much more pressing matters at hand. She turned to face him and fisted her hands on her hips. "Okay, take off your shirt."

JAKE KNEW WHAT she meant, but his mind went in a few other directions first. He was a little proud of himself for swallowing down "you first."

He raised an eyebrow, expecting her to wither a little. But she only lifted her chin. "Your arm needs to be bandaged, and I need to make sure you weren't cut anywhere else. We need to disinfect everything since you were rolling around in the back alley of a bar. And if you honestly think that I won't call a doctor because you're brushing it off like a scratch, you don't know me well enough yet."

It was probably wrong he liked that "yet" since it meant she planned for him to get to know her that well at some point.

So, he shrugged. He tossed his hat into a chair in the corner and untied the bandana he'd secured around the wound. It was soaked with blood, so he shoved it in his pocket rather than bloody up any of the hotel room. Then, ignoring the searing pain in his arm and some of the aches in his muscles from tussling, he shrugged out of his coat and then reached back and pulled his shirt off. He tossed them both on the chair. "Happy?"

She didn't say anything at first. She stood there

looking very…prim and still. He might have said detached.

But her eyes wandered.

He grinned.

Which seemed to remind her of the task at hand. "Sit," she ordered, pointing at the bed.

The one bed.

He sat. She set the first aid kit the receptionist had given her next to him on the bed, then disappeared into the bathroom. She returned with a wet washcloth and some towels.

"Don't know that we should bloody up the hotel towels."

"I'll pay the fee," she returned. She took off her hat, then busied herself opening the kit and setting some things out, then examining his wound with a critical eye. There was some kind of antiseptic wipe in the kit and she opened it, using it to wipe away the drying blood.

She sighed, her breath brushing over his arm like its own caress. "Jake, this is bad. And I can see you've had worse, but that doesn't mean we can leave this unattended."

"A day or two, we head back to the ranch. Dunne can stitch me up."

"Because Dunne is a doctor?"

He shrugged. "Close enough."

Her frown deepened, but she continued to clean him up, using a few adhesive bandages. She used quick, economical movements that told him she'd done some cleaning and patching up of other people in her day.

"You really do just take care of everyone in your path, don't you?"

She flicked her gaze up to his for a startled moment, then frowned down at the supplies, grabbing some gauze. "You're helping me. You got stabbed helping me." She let out a shaky breath, the only sign of any distress. "I think I can slap on a few bandages."

She wrapped the gauze around the bandages, which was a smart move since the wound was so deep and every bit of pressure would help the healing process.

She smoothed some tape over the gauze into place, her face still tilted down so he could see only the crown of her head.

Her fingertips brushed across the scar right above where the man had slashed his arm. "Did you get these all in the military?"

He stiffened in spite of himself, even knowing it was more than likely she'd ask about his scars. He even had the lie prepared before he'd taken off his shirt.

But he found he couldn't quite commit to those lies. "Mostly. But I was a foster kid."

She lifted her head, that frown of confusion wrinkling her forehead. "What does that mean?"

"I survived a lot of injuries in the military between training and missions." The last mission had left the biggest ones on his leg, but he'd healed a lot better than Dunne. Still, the one on his shoulder she was touching hadn't had a thing to do with the military.

"But before that…you had injuries because you were a foster kid?"

He didn't have to answer her. He didn't *have* to let her push him into this conversation. A conversation he hadn't had with anyone since it had happened. Because he'd joined the military and his life had changed. Who he was to his marrow had inextricably changed.

But Zara and this little mission they were on had nothing to do with the military, and it made him feel a bit like that kid. He wasn't in control here. He was just a person, plopped down into a different life.

Not all that different from the foster homes. Except now he had a choice. A choice to stay. To build something. No one could kick him out or tell him what to do. No more missions he didn't volunteer for. No more rules.

There was only him.

And her.

"I was staying with this family when I was seventeen. They took in kids like me, about to age out, and tried to give them some kind of…something. They were good people." He owed them a lot. Even with everything that had happened. "They usually took girls, but they'd made an exception for me for whatever reason."

He looked down at his hands, then at her. Watching him. Interested. He wasn't used to someone being interested in old truths. Not when he was in the middle of living a lie.

"The mom had an ex-husband and he showed up one night. Drunk. Violent. He had this big hunting knife, and he was going after her, so I stepped in to stop him."

"Jake." She said it on a kind of gasp that didn't quite make sense to him. Sure, it had been a bad night. But he'd heard of worse nights. He was inexorably linked to five men with similar bad nights, bad childhoods that had led them to Team Breaker.

They'd all made something good out of it.

"That was very brave," she said. "I can't imagine… They must be proud of you. Of your service and—"

He shook his head and tried to hold back the bitter laugh. It shouldn't be bitter. It was just life. "Sent me back to the home the next day. The current husband thought it meant something it didn't. That I'd step in and risk my life like that. For his wife."

"Her husband." Zara bristled. "You mean your foster *father*."

He shrugged. "Whatever. It was a bad night, and he couldn't take it out on the ex, so he took it out on me. That's okay."

"It most certainly is not."

"I was seventeen, Zara. Practically an adult."

"Hardly."

"Because you were enjoying the childish, lack-of-responsibility life when you were seventeen? Or were you playing mother to your sisters who aren't any younger than you?"

She opened her mouth, but nothing came out. Because she might not have told him that point-blank, though it didn't take a genius to connect all her dots.

"Well, you're all patched up," she said, standing. She put away the first aid items. Then she grabbed his bag and set it on the bed next to him. "You should probably change your clothes."

"Probably," he returned. Standing. Best to let it all lie. They had bigger things to deal with than discussing their pasts.

It was just… For a moment, he'd felt that glimmer

of being *human* that it felt like he'd lost as part of Team Breaker.

That was exactly why he couldn't entertain that feeling for too long. He was a liability.

He pulled some clothes out of his bag, then turned to watch her shrug off her coat.

She laid it over his discarded shirt on the chair. Which was when he saw the spots of red on the back of her blue T-shirt.

He swore and dropped his clothes. "*You're* bleeding." He stalked over to her, began to lift the back of her shirt. There were little scratches, pricks. She'd been *stabbed* and hadn't mentioned it.

She slapped at his hands, tried to turn to face him though he held her in place. "Stop that."

"Take off your shirt. *You're bleeding.*"

She slapped at him again. "I'm not going to take off my shirt in front of you."

He scowled at her, letting her go but not about to let *this* go. "Why not? You're wearing a bra, aren't you?"

Her cheeks went red again. "Of course I am."

"No offense, Zara, but I can't picture you wearing something lacy and see-through." Well, that was a lie. He could definitely picture it. He just meant he doubted his fantasy was based too much in reality. "It's no different than a bikini top."

"I would *never* wear a bikini."

He rolled his eyes. "Sit. Take off your shirt. Tit for tat, princess." That was a terrible choice of words.

She stood there, mutinous, like she was considering fighting him.

"You patched me up, and now I'm returning the

favor. I can lift your shirt up and have this take twice as long, or you can stop being a baby and sit down and take your damn shirt off."

She sneered at him, plopped herself on the bed and then finally lifted the shirt over her head. She crossed her arms over her chest.

"It's a sports bra, for goodness' sake."

She glared at him. "So what?"

"So what? I could go to a gym and see a sea of women in a lot less than that and manage to contain my baser urges."

"Baser…" She made a choking sound as her cheeks kept getting redder and redder. "That's *not* what I meant."

"Then what did you mean?"

"I don't know. It's just…weird."

"Yeah, I'll apologize when I'm feeling less furious you've been hurt this entire time and didn't tell me."

"I forgot about it."

He scoffed. He pulled the bandages back out of the kit, and some antiseptic cream. He tried to rein in his temper, but the thought of her hurt… Hurt and not telling him. Taking care of *him* first.

Who had ever done that?

She had angled herself so her back was to him. There were little scratches, deeper gashes. Nothing as bad as he'd gotten on his arm, but certainly nothing you just *forgot* about.

"What the hell happened in there? I thought I was the only one dealing with a nutjob with a knife."

"It was a woman. She came up behind me. Put the

knife to my back, told me to walk out the back door. I did at first, because…"

He sat down and used one of the towels to wipe down her wounds. "Because what?"

"She said you'd be dead if I didn't."

He stilled. And was glad her back was to him, because he had no doubt his usually carefully organized features had fallen lax in shock.

"But I figured maybe I should trust the military guy to take care of himself. But… Well, anyway. She didn't really hurt me, and the bartender came in and told her he'd called the cops. So she bolted."

It all came rushing back. Over the flashes of just surviving the man with the knife. The woman running out. *We'll come back for her later.*

He put some cream on his finger and gently rubbed it over the cuts. She jumped when the antiseptic touched her skin.

"Forgot about it, my butt," he muttered.

"It's *cold*. Not painful."

She held herself rigidly straight, arms still crossed over her chest as if she was guarding some sort of treasure. He'd been in the military too long, sharing barracks and showers and having nothing personal or private during and before his military service. It was hard to understand how different her childhood must have been.

He moved quicker, affixing bandages across all the cuts. He didn't let himself linger, or his eyes wander.

Okay, maybe once. But mostly he finished up everything quickly and stood. He grabbed her bag and handed it to her so she could put on a new shirt. She rummaged through it quickly and pulled the shirt over her head in a deft movement. He should have looked away, given her privacy, but it was all such a foreign concept.

"You have a scar on your shoulder too." He hadn't meant to say that out loud.

She finally met his gaze again. "Horse. Not human."

They stared at each other for a long while. He couldn't say why. He couldn't seem to bring himself to break the silence.

"I have the sneaking suspicion neither of us are very good at letting other people look out for us or work with us," she said finally.

His mouth curved. "Seems likely. But I think we're going to have to figure it out."

"The working-together thing."

"I meant both."

Chapter Fifteen

There was something about the way Jake held her gaze that made Zara want to run. Back to Bent. To the police. To Thomas. To whoever would get her far away from this...tight band around her lungs. This squeezing, unknown panic she didn't recognize, when she'd been very well versed in a lot of kinds of terror.

Fear was all the same, she supposed. It was something that had to be pushed aside in order to deal with the problem at hand. "These two people at the bar. They were following us. The woman mentioned my sister."

"Amberleigh or Hazeleigh?"

She let out a long, slow breath of relief. He wasn't going to push his odd...comment. "I'm not sure. It seemed like Amber. But...I can't be sure. I can't be sure of anything."

"Except they followed us. You, in particular. And wish us harm."

"Harm with knives? Why not shoot us?"

"The man I fought said something about being loud. Still, it was a risk to try and, what, kidnap you?"

Her. In particular. Not *them*. She tried to suppress a shudder.

"So, they're not exactly on a killing spree," Jake continued. "They want something from you. Something to do with Amberleigh."

"If they knew anything, they'd know I don't know *anything* about Amberleigh."

"But Hazeleigh did. She said she was safe in jail. Maybe these people were after her, and now they think you know what Hazeleigh knows." His eyebrows drew together. "So, they're after you." He swore and then grabbed her by the shoulders so suddenly she didn't know what to do but stare up at him. "You need to go back to Wilde. You need to go to Thomas or whoever. I'll handle this, but you need protection."

She tried to wiggle out of his grasp, but he held firm. His blue eyes serious and intense. So much so her first instinct was to simply agree with whatever orders he was doling out. But… "I can't do that. Everything I know makes it seem like Hazeleigh did this when I know she didn't."

"You just won't tell them what you know. I'll keep the necklace. I'll try to find these people, but—"

"We're in this together, Jake. You said that yourself. I'm not going to go hide away if you're not going to. Why should I?"

"Because *I* have experience with this."

"With hunting down murderers?" she scoffed.

He didn't falter. "More than less, Zara. Certainly far more than you."

"I am capable—"

"You are capable of everything." He gave her a little shake, frustration rippling from him in a way she'd never seen from him before. "I know that, but we're talking about someone out to *harm* you. Do you want to end up like Amberleigh?"

She had a flash of her sister, dead and buried in the dirt. Killed and discarded. Hazeleigh, pale and drawn in jail but certain she was safe there. Safe. Zara looked up at Jake. If she went back to Wilde and the police, she might be safe but Jake wouldn't be.

That felt...unendurable. That he'd be out here in danger when she was hiding. "You just said we needed to work together."

He touched her cheek. It was not...like anyone had ever touched her before. A gentleness, a reverence that had all the words and arguments in her brain simply fading away.

"I can't bear the thought of you getting hurt in this. Any more than you already have been. We'll still be working together if you go to the police. I'll still be trying to find the people who did this, and so will you. You'll just have better protection."

She wanted to reach up and touch his hand. Trace his fingers on her cheek and memorize how that fit and felt and reverberated through her. She didn't know what she was supposed to *do* with any of those wants, but they filtered through her mind like a to-do list.

Instead she only curled her hands into fists at her sides. Touching didn't seem like a reasonable response to him trying to get her out of the way. When this was her responsibility. "The only way I go to the police is if you go home."

He dropped his hands and stepped away, shoving his fingers through his hair as he turned his back to her. "Damn it, Zara."

"That's how it is," she said, terrified by all the things jangling inside of her that she didn't have the time to sort through, reason away. "Either we both retreat or we both see this through. This goes both ways, you know. The whole…" She swallowed at the tightness in her throat. It felt too much like fear to let the words go unsaid. "The whole seeing-you-get-hurt thing."

He slowly turned to face her, something like surprise or awe or anguish or all three on his face.

"So, the plan stays the way it is," Zara said firmly. She knew her voice was too high and squeaky, but she pretended she didn't notice. That she was the most in-charge person in the room. "In the morning, we go asking around. See if anyone saw Amberleigh and Hazeleigh together. Who they were with. We find the information we came for."

He gave a slight nod. "And what do we do until morning?"

There was something about the way he said "do" that had her thinking about the bed behind them. The *one* bed, and just them in this room, and the way he'd touched her face and… Well, the way he was staring at her now with all that intensity she realized he often *hid* that intensity, not that it was lacking.

Because he was an intense guy. A guy who always stepped in to protect, even when it got him hurt or kicked out of a nice foster house. He'd stepped in to help her when he'd owed her nothing. When to this very moment he owed her *nothing*.

Because it was who he was. It didn't have anything to do with her personally. He was just a…a…rescuer.

She knew the type, wasn't *she* the same type? So... It was just...him out there doing the right thing because...

I can't bear the thought of you getting hurt in this.

When she wasn't used to people giving her much of a second thought at all unless it was "how is Zara going to handle everything?"

What would they do until morning? "Sleep?" she managed to croak. And she was quite sure she turned a furious shade of red when he only grinned.

"Is THAT A QUESTION?" Jake asked, amused by the possibility of what might be going on in her head. What with the blushing and squeaking.

"N-no. We should sleep." She swallowed. Hard. Then she turned toward the bed and stared at it. "We can...take turns."

"I think I can control my baser urges. Oh wait, you're not worried about that. So, what are you worried about?"

She scowled at him. "I don't know. It's just *weird*."

Jake shrugged. "I'm sorry. You have to understand, I don't have that same...'weird' lens. Growing up in foster care, my entire adult life in the military. Things aren't...your things. Space isn't your space. You learn to make do with whatever you've got." Which was a lot more truth than he probably needed to give her, but he didn't want her to think he was *trying* to make her uncomfortable.

Even if the discomfort did kind of amuse him.

"I'm sorry," she said softly. Eyes soft. Everything *soft*.

Which made everything inside of him twist in his

own discomfort. Which was probably fair. "What's to be sorry about?"

"It sounds…"

He raised an eyebrow waiting for her response.

"Never mind. Let's just…go to sleep."

He wanted to argue, demand an answer and lots of other things he didn't fully understand churning around. But instead, he let it go.

They got ready for bed in silence. She crawled into the bed gingerly. She held herself very still, and though he didn't fully understand all of her concerns, he felt uncomfortable doing the thing she thought was "weird."

"I can sleep on the chair."

She frowned at him. "Oh, no. You can't make me feel bad and then play the noble guy."

"I didn't want to make you feel bad. I don't…"

"Just get in bed, for heaven's sake. And go to sleep." She rolled onto her side, tucked her hand under her pillow and resolutely closed her eyes.

He finally understood the idea of *weird*. Because now he knew what she looked like when she went to sleep at night. How she arranged her body, the different angles of her face when she was trying to sleep.

Knowing those things about Zara hit differently than when it was a foster brother or a fellow soldier. This was Zara, and knowing what she looked like curled up in bed…

Well, *hell*.

But he didn't have a choice now. He'd made her feel *bad*. He eased onto the bed, over the covers, wondering if it was enough of a barrier to negate the *weird*.

After a while of lying there, staring at the ceiling, she let out a gusty sigh and rolled over to face him.

"I'm exhausted, but I'll never sleep. Not when I don't understand anything that's going on. My mind will just run in circles until morning."

"So, talk out the circles. Think of it like counting sheep. Say all the possibilities until you're dead to the world."

His eyes had adjusted to the mostly dark, though a streak of streetlight pierced through the curtains and gave the room enough of a glow he could make out her features.

"Two people wanted to kidnap me. That we know."

"Yes."

"Hazeleigh thinks she's safer in jail, which means we can presume she's in danger. From these people? Are they the ones who killed Amberleigh?"

"I thought that at first, but it seems…if they killed Amberleigh, why wouldn't they just kill you too? You live on a rather isolated ranch, in that little cabin, with no real protection. And they're going through a lot of trouble to frame Hazeleigh…if they're the ones who killed Amberleigh."

"They think I know something, maybe? Some sort of information they need. But…for what?"

"The problem is, Amberleigh had a whole life away from Wilde that you don't know anything about. Now, she might have told Hazeleigh something. They might assume they told you too. But…"

"But if they want to silence me, they could have killed me when they killed Amberleigh. Hazeleigh too, for that matter."

"Maybe it's unconnected. Two separate things." But he didn't think so. He turned over everything they'd seen, been through today. What she was saying. "What if they *need* you?"

"What could they need from…?" Her eyes slowly widened as she seemed to come to the same conclusion he'd started to come to. "I look just like Amberleigh."

"I think they might need you to *be* Amberleigh for something."

She sat up suddenly, though she didn't leap from the bed. "Hazeleigh has to know. That's why she thought she'd be *safer* in jail. She knew they needed her for something. She was meeting with Amberleigh, so she probably knows what."

"She didn't tell you though."

"No, she won't. She'll consider it protecting me."

"Even if you tell her what's happened today?"

Zara took a breath, looked like she was going to say something but then just let out a slow breath.

"Ah, you won't tell her either."

"It's just… She'll worry."

He got up off the bed, too irritated with her to lie still next to her. "I mean, sure, risk your life so Hazeleigh doesn't *worry*."

"Well, don't get all angry about it."

"Angry about it?" She didn't know what angry *was*. "It's infuriating. I've spent the past ten years tethered to Cal, who does the same damn martyr stuff. You aren't the only one who can take care of things. You aren't the only one who has to suffer. I realize no one ever told you that, but you need to figure that out. All it ever does is make *you* and anyone who wants to help miserable."

"I'm not miserable."

"Aren't you?"

She looked so shocked by that, he pressed his advantage.

"We're going back to Wilde. You're going to tell Hazeleigh what happened and make her tell you what they need a body double for, if they're the ones who killed Amberleigh."

He stood there feeling unaccountably angry with her and knowing it wasn't her fault. He had Cal issues. This wasn't about her.

Except in all the ways it was.

"You're right."

And because he was used to Cal's hardheaded refusal to listen to *anything*, he was taken wholly off guard. "I am?"

She laughed, a little sadly and got out of bed. "I don't know about going back to Wilde, but you're right. I take everything on my own shoulders because I've always had to. Or thought I did. But it sure seems like Hazeleigh did the same thing. I was upset because I thought they were keeping something from me on purpose. Because I was always the triplet who was all work and no fun, who wanted to follow the rules."

She flipped on the light. She looked exhausted, dark circles under her eyes.

"But your little…outburst makes me realize… maybe it's not leaving me out. Maybe Hazeleigh is trying to protect me. But that's the thing, Jake. When you love someone, you want to protect them. She's my sister. I've been playing mom to her since we were eight. Maybe even before that. We don't want each other to worry, because…that's part of loving someone. Not wanting them to hurt."

What she didn't say, but what hung in the air between them, was that he didn't understand because he didn't have a family.

Except he did. Maybe he hadn't grown up with one, and maybe it had taken years to accept that he was stuck with the men of Team Breaker as his family, but they had become everyone who mattered to him.

And yeah, the infuriating part of Cal still playing leader after everything was that none of them wanted Cal worrying over them. They didn't want him stressing himself out over them, because they didn't want that challenge for him. Their brother.

And Jake didn't want it for Zara either. To think she had to handle this hard thing on her own.

"So, what do you want to do, Zara?" he asked, feeling tired and pummeled…a familiar feeling. Because he didn't know how to make this right for her.

Before she could answer his question, a hard knock sounded on the door.

Chapter Sixteen

Zara looked at Jake, who looked at her. Who would be knocking on their door in the middle of the night?

"Don't move," Jake said in a whisper. She didn't know where he'd stowed it, but suddenly the gun was back in his hand. He moved for the door, silently and like…someone else. He put on a mask or a costume and became someone else entirely.

She supposed it should concern her, but mostly she just felt safe. Like someone had her back. Someone saw through all her tough acts and heavy burdens and just…picked them up with her. Because…

The "because" was still a little too murky.

He was looking out the peephole. "It's your cousin," Jake said, clearly as confused as she was. "He's not in his uniform."

"Damn it, Zara." Thomas's strained voice came through the door. "I know you're in there. I came alone. Off duty. Let me in."

Jake looked back at her. Like it was her choice and he'd follow it either way. She supposed, since it was her family, it had to be her choice.

She didn't know the right one to make. But that had never allowed her the choice *not* to make the decision.

"Do you really think he's alone?"

Jake nodded.

"All right. Let him in."

Jake put the gun away first. An interesting detail, since she had no doubt Thomas would be carrying, even if he *was* off duty.

Thomas stepped in when Jake opened the door, then let it close behind him. He eyed Jake with skepticism and some very faintly veiled animosity before he turned his gaze to Zara.

"What the *hell* are you doing?"

Zara crossed her arms over her chest. Much as she might want Thomas's help or to confide in someone who might know more about the case than she did, she knew where his loyalties lay. That badge. Whether he was wearing it or not. "Maybe it's best if I don't answer that."

Thomas raked his hands through his hair. "I am not here as a cop. I am here as your cousin."

"Is there a difference? As I recall, you *arrested* Hazeleigh."

"You know *I* didn't. There is evidence against her and—"

Zara turned away from him. The fact he could still defend Hazeleigh being in a *cell*. "You should go."

"I have to talk to you. *Alone*."

She didn't have to look to know he'd be glaring pointedly at Jake. "Jake stays," Zara said firmly. "*Jake* has helped. I can't say the same for you." She knew it wasn't fair, but she was afraid if she wasn't a little unfair and mean to Thomas, she'd end up confiding in him and getting Hazeleigh into even deeper trouble.

There was a tense silence, and Zara stared at the rumpled bed. Jake had been angry with her. For wanting to do this all on her own. He'd called her a martyr and she couldn't say he was *wrong*, just that she'd never been given the opportunity to be anything but.

Until now. And not just with Jake. Could she trust Thomas? Ask for help? Let someone else shoulder the burdens?

She looked back at Jake. Because she didn't know what to do and she'd never had someone to help in that department.

She wanted someone to help in that department now and again.

Jake gave her a little nod. "It's okay. I'll take a look around the hotel. See if anyone else has followed us. I'll be back in fifteen."

When she gave her own nod in return, he slid out the door, leaving her alone with her cousin. She couldn't look at Thomas. It hurt too much. If she'd ever been forced to ask for help, Thomas was the one she would have asked.

And he'd been complicit in Hazeleigh being arrested.

"Hazeleigh told me you might be here," he said after a few quiet moments.

Zara whirled on him. "What?"

"I told her you'd up and disappeared and asked her if she knew anything about that. She was worried, Zara. Clearly, she's in danger and now you are too."

Danger, yes, and Hazeleigh apparently knew where

she'd go. Which meant Hazeleigh knew Zara would have found the letters.

Which wasn't surprising. They were triplets and lived together. They understood each other, even when they didn't act the same. But if Hazeleigh knew enough to know she was in danger, to be worried about Zara, it meant she knew way more than she was letting on. Not just to the police, but to Zara too.

"What else did she tell you?"

"Not much. I'm here because of you, Zara. You shouldn't be here at all, let alone with that *guy*. Jake Thompson isn't who he says he is. I haven't figured out who he *is*, but not who he says."

Zara knew that, didn't she? Jake had all but admitted it to her. She figured it had something to do with his military service. But none of it had to do with *this*. "Maybe not, but he doesn't have anything to do with Amberleigh. Why are you focusing on him when you should be focusing on who actually killed Amberleigh? Hazeleigh didn't. Jake didn't."

"Can you be sure of that? That Jake doesn't connect to this?"

"Yes. More than sure. I trust Jake, Thomas. I'd trust him with my life."

"Look, if this is…personal…"

The face Thomas made might have been comical if Hazeleigh wasn't in jail. If Amberleigh wasn't dead.

"This isn't about Jake. It's about getting Hazeleigh out of jail. It's about finding out who killed my sister. *Jake* is helping because…because he's a good friend."

"Helping and investigating is the police's job."

"As long as Hazeleigh is in jail, they suck at it."

"Laurel believes me." He tapped his fist to his chest. "She knows Hazeleigh didn't do it. We're looking for the real killer. I told you that. She told you that."

"And what have you got?"

"Since Grady told me—and Laurel—everything he saw at the bar, we've got the two people who attacked you and Jake to go on."

Grady must be the bartender who'd helped her. The detective's husband. Which was good, all in all, if the cops were looking for people who'd attacked them. It would be harder for her would-be kidnappers to get to her. She hoped.

"Laurel is looking into this," Thomas continued. "She won't be far behind, and no, I didn't tell her anything about coming here or Hazeleigh telling me you'd be here. I'm just saying, she's smart. She's going to put it together."

"Well, when she does, maybe you can arrest the people who attacked me instead of my sister."

He groaned in frustration. "Do you really think I want Hazeleigh in jail?"

"No, I don't." She swallowed down the wave of guilt. "But I think if the evidence points to her being guilty, you'd let it happen. It's your job to let it happen."

"It's my job to help enforce the truth."

She felt sorry for him, even though she wanted to harden her heart against it. He was in an impossible situation. She knew how hard he'd worked to become a cop. How much it meant to him. Now he was being torn between what he'd dedicated his life to and his family.

"Go enforce the truth then, Thomas," she said, trying to firm her voice against the way it wanted to shake with emotion. "Leave me be. Some of us put family above all else. If that isn't you, you can go."

He looked at her a bit like she'd shot him, but Zara didn't have time to feel guilty about that. The door opened and Jake slid back inside in absolute silence. But he immediately crossed to her, and she could tell no matter how stoic he tried to act, he was a bit rattled.

"You've got to get out of here," Jake said, taking her arm and already moving her toward the door.

She dug her heels in out of reflex. "What? Why?"

"The two people from the bar are out there in the parking lot. They are not alone."

JAKE GRABBED ZARA'S bag with his free hand and shoved it at Thomas. "Get her out of here. I'll create a diversion."

"No," Zara said, still trying to wriggle out of his grasp.

He held firm. "You need to get somewhere safe. We know they want you. I don't plan on letting them get you."

"Explain that," Thomas ordered.

"It's noth—"

"The theory we're working on is that they need Zara for something," Jake interrupted, not about to let Zara play it off like it was nothing. Not when she'd been *stabbed* in the back in a kidnap attempt. "Like impersonating Amberleigh, maybe." Jake understood Zara's reticence to trust Thomas, but in the current circumstance, he was her best shot at getting out of here in one piece *and* getting somewhere safe. Maybe to a jail cell like her sister.

"Why would they need that?" Thomas asked.

"*That* we don't know. But they wanted to kidnap Zara, not kill her. At least right now. Hazeleigh feels safer in a cell than at home. The common denominator isn't what they know. If Hazeleigh has much more information about Amberleigh's past than Zara does, the commonality is the face."

"All I need to do is call someone in," Thomas said. "You can identify the woman who attacked you and so can Grady. We'll arrest her and see what she knows. It doesn't have to be all dark-alley schemes."

"I'm not dealing with the police," Zara said, crossing her arms over her chest. She gave a sideways look at her bag that Jake sure hoped Thomas didn't catch on to. Because that bloody necklace in Zara's bag was a big problem.

"I know you're ticked Hazeleigh is in jail, but the police can and will help. We will *help*. And do the right thing. If you'd stop playing at vigilante, we can figure this out."

"Oh, can we?"

"Call the cops if you have to," Jake interrupted. "Do what you've got to do, but she has to be out of here. I can take her or you can."

"Do I get a say?" Zara asked, dangerously casual.

"No," he said in unison with Thomas. Then they both winced, as if they'd realized at the same time they'd made a grave tactical error.

"So, to be clear, you plan on carting me around like a *child* while I let the big, strong men handle things?"

"Zaraleigh—"

She sent Thomas a cutting look.

"They are after *you*," Jake said, trying to keep his fury and worry leashed. "It's not about men and women. It's not about anything except the fact they want *you* and we are trying to keep that from happening."

Zara finally tugged hard enough he let go of her arm. "They want me." She seemed to consider that as she crossed to the window. She looked out for a while and Jake had to battle against the impatience to get her far away from those people downstairs.

Eventually she turned to face him and Thomas. "Why not let them have me? It would answer our questions. I'd just…do whatever they asked. Then we'd know what they want me for."

Jake laughed. Thomas sputtered. Then they both said the same thing at the same time.

"No."

"And," Zara continued as if this was somehow a plausible or reasonable course of action. "Thomas and his cops can arrest them for kidnapping me after. Not only does it give us answers, but also it puts them in jail."

"I can already have her arrested for assault. I don't need your kidnapping plan."

"Jake said there's more than just the woman. A whole group of people who might have answers about what happened to Amberleigh. Don't we want all of them?"

"Not if it puts you in danger," Jake said before Thomas could.

She stood there, looking angry and frustrated, but

she didn't keep arguing. She wasn't the kind of woman who beat her head against a brick wall.

She was the kind of woman who figured her way up and around it.

"Fine," Zara said. "Call your cops. Arrest the woman and just the woman." She shrugged. "I have to go to the bathroom." She turned and disappeared into the bathroom, the lock clicking shut.

"I don't trust her for a second," Thomas muttered. "There's not a window or a way out in there, is there?"

"No."

"Good. Keep an eye on her." Thomas pulled his phone out of his pocket and stepped into the hallway, free hand on the butt of the weapon he clearly wore under his coat.

Jake watched the bathroom door. There weren't any other exits *in* the bathroom, but he didn't trust her either. He had a very bad feeling he knew just what she was up to.

And that he'd go along with it, simply because she was going to ask him to.

She poked her head out of the bathroom, looking around the room, likely for Thomas. "He gone?"

"Just out in the hallway."

She gave a sharp nod. "Okay, here's the plan."

Chapter Seventeen

"I'm not going to get in the way of him arresting her, if that's why you're scowling," Zara said, moving over to her bag.

"Oh, good. So there is some reasonable part to your plan?"

He sounded sarcastic, so she glared at him. "But that leaves how many people out there who presumably want to get their hands on me? Or my face anyway?"

"Four. And I'll be damned if I'm going to let that happen. Sorry."

"It'd be easier. Quicker." Frustrating to be thwarted by do-gooder men, but she'd deal. She didn't exactly *want* to be kidnapped, but much like back at the bar, she realized she was willing to do a lot of things she didn't want to in order to get to the bottom of this. "We'll follow them instead."

"Follow them," he repeated, as if it was just as insane as letting herself be kidnapped.

She checked on the bloody necklace. Still there. Still a problem. She thought about handing it over to Thomas. He was here in an unofficial capacity.

But he was calling the cops in. He wasn't bending

any rules. He was just getting in the way. She zipped her bag and turned to face Jake. "They followed us. Why can't we follow them?"

"Because they're potential murderers?"

"There's also potentially more of them out there? All after me maybe? Or Hazeleigh? We don't know, and the cops keep focusing on one little thing at a time. Them arresting the *one* woman who tried to kidnap me does nothing."

Jake didn't say anything to that, and she knew it wasn't for lack of *trying* to come up with something to say. It was just he had to know she was right.

"You'll tell Thomas that you're taking me back to Wilde to keep me away from these folks. Keep playing up the macho, I-know-better-than-the-little-girl act, and he'll eat it up."

"That's not what that was," he returned, scowling. "I'm very aware you can take care of yourself. On a ranch. In life. But we're talking about murderers here. We're talking about the very real possibility you get hurt. *Again.*"

"If I get hurt in the process, at least I did something to help."

"And if you're dead in the process?"

"How do I just go around knowing someone killed my sister? Knowing someone wants Hazeleigh to take the fall for that? The police haven't gotten as far as we have."

"Because they don't have all the information."

"Are you suggesting we give them all the information?"

He inhaled. "No. But… Thomas seems to want to help."

"By the book. The book sucks."

His mouth curved just a little bit. "You would have made a decent addition to Team Breaker, Zara."

"What's Team Breaker?"

"Something I really shouldn't have mentioned. There are things you don't know about me."

He said it so seriously. Holding her gaze. As if there was something *bad* about that, something to apologize for.

But she'd meant what she'd said to Thomas. She trusted this man with her life. "Wow. So surprising, Jake," she said with a roll of her eyes in an attempt to take some tension out of the room. "However will I cope?"

His mouth quirked again. "So, we say I'm taking you back to Wilde. We follow whoever scatters when the police come. And then what?"

"We see where they go. We see if it gives us answers."

"And if it doesn't?"

She searched for a next step. For *something*. But she came up empty. She shrugged, hating that she felt lost all over again. It seemed every time she latched on to the next step, things got murkier and murkier. "I don't know."

He nodded like that was okay, but before he could say anything, Thomas stepped back into the room.

"I've got a couple county deputies responding, and Laurel is going to come question the woman. We'll need to bring you into the station to give a statement."

"I'll take her back to Wilde," Jake said, his gaze never leaving hers. "You can trust me."

He was lying, for her. And though he was saying those words *to* Thomas, he was saying them while looking into *her* eyes.

"Straight to the station. No detours. If you don't arrive in twenty minutes, I'll be coming after you myself."

Zara forced herself to look away from Jake and to her cousin. She hated breaking his trust like this, but she hated Hazeleigh in jail and being framed more. "Can I run home real quick and check on things at the ranch? It'll only add on another twenty or so."

"Have one of the Thompson brothers do it," Thomas replied. "Twenty minutes. Now, I'm going to stay here and watch our friends from the window until one of our marked cars arrive. You two get to the station. Tw—"

"Twenty minutes. We got it." Zara headed for the door, Jake opening it for her.

"Be safe," Thomas said, so seriously she had to fight away the jolt of guilt. But maybe when this was all over, he'd understand. She sure hoped he would.

She managed a wan smile and left the room, Jake close behind her. Once again they were silent on the elevator ride down. They stepped out into the hall. Zara didn't see anyone, but as they turned the corner to the back exit, suddenly she was being pushed, nudged, led and then cornered behind a big potted plant next to the elevators.

It was the strangest thing because Jake was basically pressing her up against the wall. With his *body*.

She should probably ask him what he was doing, but

no sound came out of her mouth. His face was hovering over hers. Close. Way, way too close.

"Just don't say anything for a few minutes," he whispered, his breath fluttering over her mouth.

Her *mouth*.

A strange need to giggle rose up inside of her. Which made *no* sense. Except his mouth was just…there. Really, really close to hers. Wasn't that funny?

Except his eyes were so very blue and he positively blocked out the entire rest of the world with the sheer size of him and this…this…*feeling*. The kind she usually avoided, because *feelings* led to more responsibility, more people to take care of.

And yet Jake was never someone who added responsibility to her shoulders, was he?

"That detective just walked in," he whispered.

The *detective*. The problem at hand. Hazeleigh in jail and Amberleigh dead.

"How'd she get here so fast?" Zara started to turn her head to look, but Jake shifted, angling his body, his mouth moving closer to hers.

His *mouth*.

"Look, I'm sorry, but this is about the only thing I can think of."

Before she could ask him what that meant, his mouth was on hers.

JAKE KEPT THINKING there had to be another way to do this, but in the end, there wasn't. That detective was striding down the hall, and while she *might* take a second look at two people making out in the hallway, she likely had more important things on her mind.

Nor would she expect two people running around trying to solve a murder to have time for hallway make-out sessions.

But that meant he was kissing Zara. And as much as it was a ruse to avoid the detective's attention, his mouth was on her mouth and he couldn't seem to resist falling into a *real* kiss.

He didn't have to cover her cheek with his hand to angle her face better. He didn't have to indulge in the feel of her lips, her body pressed to his. He didn't have to taste her and torture himself with that new carnal knowledge.

He shouldn't have forgotten where they were or what they were doing for ticking seconds, where it seemed to be only them and this.

He certainly shouldn't be thinking of possibilities. Of what he wanted. If he was someone else, what he wanted might matter. If he was someone else…

But he wasn't. He pulled himself back. He hadn't been sent to Wilde to build a life, even if that's what he wanted to do. He'd been sent to Wilde to hide. He'd never be able to tell her why, and he was already risking too much just by being here.

He stayed close but fully pulled his mouth from hers. She blinked up at him, mouth slightly agape. Dark eyes wide and, well, certainly not angry or offended.

A strange panic settled over him. A flustered feeling he thought he'd eradicated from his life after that first foster home didn't work out.

"That was just a…" There was a word he was searching for. Somewhere inside of his melted brain. He cleared his throat. "I figured she wouldn't look too closely at two people making out in the hallway. What with the danger and death and all."

Zara didn't move. Didn't say a word. And they couldn't stay here with cops on their way, and the group outside being able to leave at any second.

"We have to go." He took her by the arm and started pulling her toward the door. Still, she said nothing, but she followed.

He stopped at the door, studying the dark parking lot out the glass of the back door. He didn't see anyone from this angle, but they still had to be careful.

He didn't drop her hand. He kept her close. As his heart beat painfully from every emotion that kiss had stirred up, he forced his brain to focus on the mission.

Because the mission was keeping her safe, and that was everything.

They walked to his truck, sticking to the shadows. Jake heard low voices. He moved, keeping Zara behind him, acting as a physical barrier between her and where he thought the voices were coming from. The group he'd spotted on his first perusal was standing in the same place, though now one of the trucks they were standing next to was running.

He didn't have to tell Zara they needed to be utterly silent. They inched toward his truck, keeping each footfall absolutely silent. When they reached his truck, he used his key to manually unlock the driver's side door. The group was a good ways away, but it would only take one to see his dome light go on.

He put his mouth next to Zara's ear. "We're going to stand here and not get in until they leave. We'll watch which way their headlights go and follow at a good distance. We have to be careful and stay far enough back they won't notice someone following them in the middle of the night, in the middle of nowhere."

She nodded. He could feel the brush of her hair against his jaw. He had the overpowering need to bundle her up, shove her in the truck, take her back to the ranch and lock her in her cabin so he could take care of this himself.

She'd never go for it. He understood that, but it didn't mean he could get rid of the impulse to take care of this *for* her.

Sirens sounded in the distance and Zara jerked a little bit. Jake gave her hand a squeeze. Reassurance. A reminder to stay still and quiet.

Connection.

The group in the front lot looked around, clearly a little worried about the source and reason for those sirens. Coming closer. Jake held himself very still, again keeping Zara behind him so if they *did* make him out in the shadows, they didn't see her.

Three men got into the running truck and began to pull away. The two people left tried to get into the cab, but the truck screeched away without them. Jake could hear their muttered curses as they began to run. Maybe toward a car of their own.

But they were stopped, just before they were out of Jake's line of sight, by Laurel and Thomas. The man tried to punch Thomas, and Zara gasped, so Jake squeezed her hand tighter as a reminder to be quiet.

Laurel had the woman in handcuffs as a police cruiser with lights and sirens on pulled into the front lot and then out of view.

Enough commotion Jake thought they could get going and hopefully catch up with the truck—that clearly left the would-be kidnappers behind on purpose.

He opened the door, pushed Zara inside. She quickly scurried over the driver's side to the passenger seat. He hopped in and immediately turned the ignition. He didn't peel out. He drove slowly and carefully behind the hotel.

"They took a right out of the lot, yeah?"

"Yeah," Zara agreed. She pulled her phone out. "We can't go around front." She pulled up a map as Jake eased his truck toward the street connected to the back lot. "Take a left here. We can circle around. Hopefully catch up."

"Got it."

"Why did that truck of guys leave them behind?" she asked before telling him to take another left.

"Buys them time. But it certainly points to a bigger operation." He slid her a look. "We could leave it to the police."

She stared straight ahead. "I can't."

"Understood." He followed the rest of her directions back to the highway. It was the middle of the night in the middle of nowhere. He had to be…beyond careful.

He pulled onto the highway—a deserted two-laner, the kind of nothing road he was still getting used to after over a month of living in Wyoming. In the far distance, he could just make out the taillights of a truck like the one that had pulled out of the hotel.

He couldn't be sure it was the same truck, but everything was so deserted it was unlikely to be anyone else.

Zara said nothing, and Jake couldn't think of anything to say. Not even to ask her what she thought they were going to do once the men in the truck stopped wherever they were going to stop.

He could take on three men. He'd done it before. But he was worried wherever they were headed would have more. He shifted, pulled his phone out of his pocket and shot off a quick text to all five men back at the ranch.

Track me. SOS means backup.

Maybe he shouldn't involve them, but… He couldn't keep living his life tethered to a military he couldn't be a part of anymore. At some point, he had to have his own life. Even if it had been made up for him by the military.

This was his life now. *Their* life now. Why couldn't they still do some good with it?

He kept driving, watching the taillights. He didn't know this area well, but he was pretty sure that truck could drive down this highway for hours on end and not really end up anywhere. Eventually they'd need gas. Food. Sleep.

But for now, he just followed through pitch-black night.

"I have one non-danger-related question," Zara said after a while.

"Okay."

She was quiet for a long moment while he waited. When she spoke, it was in a rush.

"I get the whole kiss-so-she-wouldn't-look-too-closely-at-us thing, but I'm not sure she was looking closely enough you had to put your tongue in my mouth."

He choked even though there was nothing in his mouth. "Sorry," he managed to croak through a coughing fit.

"I'm not looking for an apology," she said, sounding irritated with him.

"What are you looking for?"

"An explanation."

"Of why I kissed you?"

She sighed heavily, like *he* was the one not making any sense. "You're hot, Jake."

"O…kay?"

"Hot guys don't generally kiss me. I realize you were playing a part and all, but you didn't have to get *that* into it—"

"Hold on a sec. Do you think you're…not hot?"

"I mean, I can be cute like…when I brush my hair, and maybe put on non-ranch clothes, but those days are few and far between."

He didn't dare take his eyes off the truck lights so far ahead of them, so easily lost. But he shook his head and tried to put what he felt into his voice if not into his expression. "Zara, you're beautiful. Hair brushed or not."

She was quiet again. When she finally spoke, it was softly. And with that rare hint of being off-kilter. "I don't know what to say to that."

"I don't think you have to say anything."

"It's just Amberleigh was always the attractive one, and Hazeleigh the pretty one."

He wasn't sure he'd ever guess all the twists and turns her mind made. "You all look alike."

"Sure, but they try. You know, makeup and dresses and brushed hair." She waved a hand in the air in front of her. "I've known all the same people my whole life. They have all looked at me the same way my whole life. I guess I see myself the way they see me, and you see me differently…kind of. So I don't understand you. You don't need anything from me."

"Am I supposed to?"

"That's the part I don't understand. I don't have people like that in my life. You're here and doing all this and *kissing me* really well and I don't know how to reconcile all that."

"Well, as long as I'm kissing well."

She sighed. "I'm glad you think this is *so* funny."

"I'm not making it a joke. It's not a joke. I just…" He stared at the taillights. At that symbol of all the danger they were walking into. All the involvement he was supposed to avoid but hadn't been able to because it was…*her*.

There'd been something about *her* since he'd walked onto that ranch and she'd scowled at all of them. So furious they'd bought *her* ranch. But teaching them anyway. Taking care of everything anyway, because that's who she was.

He'd held back because he was supposed to. Because the military dictated it. Well, he was tired of it.

"I like you, Zara. I care about you. I'm attracted to you. I *want* to help you, because it's right. But more than that, because I don't like seeing you hurting."

He couldn't look at her, no matter how badly he wanted to. Those taillights were his only focus right now. But he couldn't stop himself. He gave her a quick once-over.

In the dark, he couldn't make out every nuance of her expression. He could only tell she held herself very still. Like she always did when she wasn't quite sure what road to go down next.

But that was the beauty of Zara. She never stayed there long. She made a choice, and she followed that road until the next choice. No waffling. No wondering. Just forward movement.

That he understood.

"Zara?"

"I don't see the taillights anymore," she said, her voice sounding very far away.

Which was just as well, since she was right. The lights had disappeared. Somewhere up ahead, the truck had pulled off the highway.

Chapter Eighteen

Zara didn't know why her eyes were all teary, why her throat felt tight. Why she couldn't seem to think beyond his words.

I like you, Zara. I care about you. I'm attracted to you. I want *to help you because it's right. But more than that, because I don't like seeing you hurting.*

That list…

Of course someone would feel all those things for her while she was trying to solve her sister's murder while her other sister was in jail. A bloody necklace in her bag. The timing made far more sense than the man.

Beautiful. No one had called her beautiful in her entire life, even on the rare occasion when she had pointed out that she had the same face as Amberleigh and Hazeleigh who were considered far more *feminine* and *desirable* than rough-and-tumble Zara had ever been.

What a bizarre thing to think about when real danger lay ahead.

"Look out for turnoffs on your side. I'll watch for them on mine. They weren't more than a mile head of us, so if we don't see anything for a mile, we'll flip around and try again until we find an option," Jake said.

He was different again. Serious. Focused. Like he could just fold up everything they'd been talking about and set it aside.

She supposed that really was the only option. So, she focused on the dark world around them and watched for a turnoff. She also thought about where they'd been driving. They were still in Bent County, but there weren't really any towns out this way. A few older ranches and some rich-folk spreads—usually vacation homes. A strange area for a bunch of people who'd possibly killed her sister.

Except it was isolated. Though she could think of more isolated spots. Better places to hide a murder. But Amberleigh had been buried on the Hart ranch. What sense did that make?

None of this made any sense.

"There," Zara said, pointing at a gravel turnoff.

Jake slowed his truck and pulled off the highway onto the gravel shoulder. He turned off his headlights and they both looked down the gravel road for signs of lights or life. Nothing Zara could make out in the dark.

Jake reached into the backseat and rummaged around in his bag. He pulled out a flashlight, and though she didn't see it, she had no doubt he had his gun somewhere on him.

"Stay put."

"Jake—" She had the strangest impulse to reach out and hold on to him. Keep him here in the truck where it was safe.

But was anywhere safe?

Jake met her gaze and smiled. "Just stay put for one minute. Just one. Promise."

She nodded, unable to voice any response. She believed his promises. That he thought she was beautiful. That he cared. She didn't know why she believed all that, only that she felt it in her bones.

So, she waited and watched carefully as his flashlight bobbed outside the truck. She didn't know what he was looking for—what she thought they might find, following these people connected to her would-be kidnappers. She supposed like every step so far, there was no way of knowing until they found it.

They.

He'd kissed her. Not just a distraction kiss. In that moment afterward, when he'd stared at her in a kind of shock, he'd seemed just as taken aback as she had been. It was a comfort, in some ways, to know he wasn't at all certain what *this* was.

Maybe uncertainty wasn't such a bad thing. Maybe it was okay to take things one second at a time before making the next choice.

After a minute and not much longer, he got back in the car. "They definitely went down this lane. There's fresh tire marks in the snow. Deep, not iced over or windswept."

"Should we go down it?"

"We follow down this isolated gravel road, even with our headlights off, we're asking for trouble. Bring up that map of yours."

She pulled out her phone and the map of the area. Jake studied it. "No other roads lead down there. Do you have any idea what's back there?"

Zara squinted into the absolute country dark. The area seemed vaguely familiar to her, but she couldn't put her finger on why. *Killroy Lane.* "I feel like I've been here before, but I don't know why. If it doesn't connect to any other roads, it's likely a drive back to a ranch or a house."

"We could walk it," Jake mused. "Still dangerous but less conspicuous. Problem is, it seems pretty long. We could be walking till daylight, and we don't know if we'll have cover."

Zara kept staring out the window, willing herself to remember why this all felt familiar. Something random. When her life was never random. She had the ranch and she had...

"Wait." She squinted into the dark. "When you were out there, did you see a mailbox?"

"Yeah. It was weird. Like a circle."

"Like a golf ball?"

"Oh, yeah. I guess so." He nodded. "Yeah, a golf ball."

Pieces started to domino in her head. It still didn't make sense, but she knew where she was. She reached out and clutched his arm. "I *know* that mailbox. I've been here. There's a house at the end of the road."

"Whose house?"

"This guy Hazeleigh dated. It was...last year I guess? This is his family's, like, summer home or something. If I'm remembering right, they don't live here full-time. He had a pool party, and Hazeleigh brought me along even though I repeatedly told her anyone who had a *pool* in Wyoming needed their head examined. But Hazeleigh doesn't really like to drive very far away, so she wanted me to go with her."

Jake was frowning. "When did Hazeleigh stop seeing him?"

"Right before last Christmas. He didn't take it well either. He called her constantly. Showed up at our house a few times. I chewed him out, even had Thomas go talk to him. The harassment stopped a few days after that, and I sort of forgot about it. Haze has never had the best taste in guys."

Zaraleigh looked at Jake. It seemed important to put it out there. "Amberleigh's first letter. It said it was almost Christmas. So, he stopped bothering her right around the time Amberleigh's letters started."

JAKE DIDN'T KNOW what to make of Zara's story. Except that he'd like to march down the lane and pop the guy one for harassing poor, skittish Hazeleigh and making Zara play protector yet again.

Of course, maybe he was *why* Hazeleigh was skittish.

Still, the timing fit too well with everything else they were trying to figure out. Amberleigh was the center. "Is there any way this guy had anything to do with Amberleigh running away back when you were teenagers?"

Zara frowned, clearly trying to comb back through years of memories. "I don't know how he would have. His family is from the county but not from Wilde. He's a doctor and Hazeleigh met him when she took Mr. Field into the emergency room one day when he was having heart troubles. The doctor asked her out, then they dated for…six months, tops. She liked him but said he was too intense."

Zara let out a breath of frustration. "It seems like it should connect, but I don't understand how. What would the letters have to do with Hazeleigh breaking up with this guy? And he wasn't one of those guys who got in the truck. He's a *doctor*. He wouldn't be loitering in a hotel parking lot in the middle of the night. He fancies himself *very* sophisticated, and he is a bit of a big fish in a small pond."

Exactly the type who would *hire* people to do their dirty work in Jake's estimation.

"So, he harassed Hazeleigh for weeks. Then the letters from Amberleigh start and his bothering you guys stops."

"I don't know, Jake. I did sic the police on him. Maybe that's what it really took. Maybe it's a coincidence."

Normally he'd agree with Zara, and he knew it was a possibility. But too much coincidence usually meant something else going on. Even if it wasn't something Jake could untangle. "What's this guy's name?"

"Douglas Nichols. *Dr.* Douglas Nichols." She rolled her eyes, clearly not a fan of the guy. "He works at Bent County Hospital."

Jake looked him up on his phone, but his signal was too weak for the results to come up quickly enough. He muttered a curse under his breath. "Someone needs to ask Hazeleigh about it. About him, specifically. And the timing with the letters from Amberleigh."

"Well, we did tell Thomas we were going to the station." Zara glanced at the clock on the dash. Way more than twenty minutes had passed. "He likely has since sent out someone to look for us."

Jake glanced out the window, toward the gravel road. He saw the faintest flash of light. It might have been nothing. A falling star. A reflection of something else.

But it looked like the flare of a match.

Jake reached over and gently pushed Zara's head down, so if someone was out there, they wouldn't be able to see her. *Or shoot her.* "Get down."

"What is it?"

He felt the flashback creeping in. Shattered images in his mind, but he also knew he didn't have time for that right now. In a moment like this, he had to use the coping mechanisms he'd learned to separate the two things in his mind.

Because this was too important. Zara was too important.

The flare of a match in Syria. The flare of a match here in Wyoming. Two different moments. Two different situations. But he had to protect people in both.

He kept his hand gently resting on Zara's head. Both to keep her down, away from the windows, and to keep himself tethered to the moment. Zara. Wyoming. Here. Now.

There was an odd *pop* sound, and the slight jerk of the truck.

Someone had shot out a tire.

He didn't understand. He'd just been outside and hadn't heard or seen anything. Now there were people shooting out their tires? And he'd *felt* her jerk right along with the truck, so he wasn't in full flashback, leaving reality behind.

"Okay, Zara, listen to me. I once took down five men who very much wanted to kill me. All on my own.

Without a gun. I tell you that so you understand. So, you don't argue with what I'm about to say. You just agree. Because I've done stuff like this before. Okay?"

"I'm going to hate this."

"Yeah, no doubt. I'm going to go out there. I'm going to fight whoever is out there, debilitate them. While I'm doing that, I want you to run."

"Jake—"

"You kind of know where we are. You have the best chance of running somewhere safe, somewhere away from this place. You call Thomas. You tell him everything. This doctor. The bloody necklace. Everything. We don't have time to argue. I just need you to go the minute I start fighting them."

"They have *guns*."

"Someone does, yes. But it's dark, and I know how to fight in the dark. I can do this, Zara." But he knew that no matter how skilled he was, it only took a moment. He fished his phone out of his pocket and shoved it at her. "If something happens, hit send on this text."

"I can't take your phone. How will we contact each—" Another pop, another jerk of the tire.

"We can't drive now. The tires are shot. Someone's likely getting closer." Someone or ones. "Can you shoot a gun?"

"Of course."

Thank God for ranch women. "There's one in the glove compartment. Grab it just in case. Then run. Trust me. You trust me, right?"

Her head nodded under his hand.

"When I close the door, count to thirty, then run." He eased the door open and listened to the night around them. He eased it closed with a quiet *snick* that seemed to echo loudly. He used the truck as a shield as he moved, trying to figure out where the shooter was coming from and how many men he might be up against.

He heard the crunch of snow in front of him, but on Zara's side.

He shoved his hands in his pockets. He found a stray screw he'd shoved into his coat pocket back at the ranch yesterday. He gave it a toss. Then he crouched down and listened as the footsteps pivoted and then headed for where the screw had landed.

So far, just one set of footsteps. Jake listened hard for anyone else close by but didn't hear anything. So when the man came around the back of the truck, Jake lunged and knocked him down. Thankfully, the big gun the man had been holding fell with a soft *plop* out of his hands and into the snow.

Jake couldn't listen for Zara. He could only hope she'd followed his instructions as he fought the man underneath him. They both grappled, punched and tried to grab the gun the man had dropped.

The guy got a decent gut punch in, but that only ticked Jake off. He landed a hard, sudden jab to the temple, knocking the guy out. Jake gave it a second, made sure the guy stayed limp and it wasn't an act.

When he was certain he'd incapacitated the man, he got up and grabbed the dropped gun. Now he had a weapon. He didn't know how long he'd have with the guy knocked out, but at least Jake was the one with the gun now. A barrier between the house and any other men that might come and Zara, running in the opposite direction.

He moved toward the gravel road, surprised to find no one else approaching. No flashes of light. No signs of life. Where had that *one* guy come from? Maybe Jake shouldn't have knocked him out and gotten some answers instead.

But there'd be answers down that road if he went down it. If Zara had listened, had run away and called Thomas, she'd have help. Maybe it was worth the risk to see if he could get her some answers.

He took a step down the road. It was pitch-black. He could only feel his way as he moved through the snow. He could only listen to the muffled sounds of a winter country night.

Maybe he should turn back. Find Zara. Make sure she was okay. She was the priority, wasn't she? Above answers. Above everything. It was cold and snowy and...

He realized someone was there in the dark with him too late. So late he didn't even have time to fight off the sudden jab of metal to his back.

"Drop it," a low voice growled.

It was always the wrong move to worry about someone else. To put someone else's well-being above your own. It led to mistakes. Just like this one.

Still, it was only one guy. Jake just had to play it right. So he didn't wince, barely even scowled. He slowly raised his hands, though he didn't drop his gun. Not just yet. Someone who could move that quietly, that stealthily had to have seen combat. "Former military too, huh?" he asked, trying to sound relaxed and casual.

"I wouldn't worry about it if I were you." The gun

jabbed into his back. "Drop the gun and state your business."

His *business*? "I was lost. Looking at the map in my car and your guy blew out my tires."

"Not my guy." He jabbed the gun harder into Jake's back. "Drop your weapon."

Reluctantly, Jake lowered and placed the gun carefully on the snow. Not *his* guy. Was the gunman lying, or were there two dangerous groups out here?

"What were you doing out here?"

"Just driving, man."

The gunman scoffed. "Maybe you're a cop."

Jake laughed. "I don't think so. Pretty sure the cops want me."

"Why'd you stop in front of this guy's house?"

"This a house? I just stopped. Figured out I was lost when I hadn't seen a town in a while. Pulled to the side of the road. Got my map out—"

"You mean the lady you were with got her map out."

This time Jake couldn't control his body. It stiffened against his will at the mention of Zara.

"You've been following us since the motel," the gunman said. "We don't like being followed."

So this was one of the guys from the parking lot. "Don't know what you're talking about."

"Well, since we had someone following you, I'd think you would. You can tell your doctor friend that his sad attempts at turning this around on us aren't going to go the way he thinks. Well, if I let you tell him anything."

The doctor? This guy thought he was connected to the doctor? He wasn't sure if it was better to go along or disabuse him of the notion or something else entirely. But if they were ever going to find out the real truth, Jake was going to have to take some chances.

"Not here about the doctor," Jake said, trying to match the way this man spoke. Prove they were one and the same. "I'm here about the dead woman."

"Don't know if you're playing dumb, or you think I am, but the doctor's got everything to do with the dead woman. Don't let him tell you otherwise, bud. Because I'm not taking the fall for him. I wouldn't even let you take the fall for him after what he did to Amberleigh. Of course, I could always kill you and let him take the fall for both."

Surely this guy didn't mean the doctor had killed Amberleigh. He just meant… Well, if Hazeleigh was being framed, maybe this guy was too.

Headlights appeared on the highway. A truck pulled up behind his. Two men got out. They killed the engine but left the lights on.

Nothing good could happen in the dark, but Jake had a bad feeling with these three guys, the light would be even worse.

Chapter Nineteen

Zara had listened to Jake's instructions.

At first.

She'd gotten out of the car, run in the opposite direction of the doctor's house as Jake grappled with some guy. She'd trusted him to handle it, no matter how it made her throat tight and her nerves jangle like little live wires all over her body.

But when she'd pulled out her phone to call Thomas, she realized she'd lost all cell service somewhere along the way. In order to find some, she'd have to retrace her steps. She could keep going, but she'd easily get lost and there was *nothing* around here except snow. Back to the highway was her best bet.

So she'd turned around and started moving slowly and carefully, back toward the truck where she knew she had at least one bar to get a phone call or text through to Thomas.

Thomas would be looking for them anyway. She held on to that. Still, she knew she needed to make contact so he knew *where* to look. She'd led Jake into something she shouldn't have, and that was on her shoulders. No matter how willingly he'd followed.

Then there'd been headlights, and she'd taken a dive into the ditch on the other side of the highway than they'd been parked on. She'd peeked up over the cold ground and watched two men get out of a truck and stride toward…

Now that there were headlights, she could see. Jake's truck's shot-out tires. The stupid golf ball mailbox. The gravel road.

And Jake. With a gun in his back. Two more men with guns approaching.

He'd said he'd once fought off *five* men when he'd been unarmed, and he wasn't the kind of guy to make up or exaggerate war stories. He was the kind who didn't have to.

Maybe she should trust that he could handle it.

But she couldn't *stand* it. Him standing there because of her. Three guns pointed at him. No matter how relaxed he looked.

She tightened her grip—not on her cell phone, but on the gun she'd gotten out of the glove compartment. Now that she had light and could see what was going on, she had a chance to help. Maybe Jake *could* fight off three men with guns while he had none, but she had one. She could give him a hand.

She only had a second, she knew. Once one shot went off, hell would break loose, and quite possibly these men would begin to shoot too. But if she could get two quick shots and disarm two of the men, then trust Jake to take out the third on his own, maybe they could get out of this.

The first and most important target was the man with the gun jabbed into Jake's back. She tested the weight of her gun, glad it was close to the kind of gun she was used to shooting. She had so little margin for error.

But in the wild world of things she didn't know, there were a few things she trusted herself with infinitely. Cows and ranching, mostly, but she also knew how to shoot a gun with pinpoint precision because she'd always wanted to be able to protect her family out there in the middle of nowhere and she'd known Dad wouldn't always be reliable in a dangerous situation.

She took a deep breath and steadied herself. She focused on the arm the man was holding his gun with. She'd aim for his arm, then the man on Jake's right's leg. She'd hope and pray he could take out the one on his left on his own.

She counted her breaths, tried to find a stillness, even with her nerves strung far too tightly.

One, two.

One, two.

She pulled the trigger once. Moved slightly. Twice. She couldn't pay attention to the results. She had to shoot and duck.

And pray.

It was a quick prayer, just *please, please, please*, before she popped up and looked at the scene below.

Three men slumped on the ground, and Jake standing over them. He looked like he was speaking to them, maybe. Zara adjusted her grip on the gun and then began to move forward.

When she approached the men, Jake frowned at her. "You were supposed to run."

She shrugged. "I ran. Then I came back."

He shook his head, then looked back down at the men on the ground. He'd collected all of their weapons. One was passed out cold, one was writhing around holding his leg, and the other looked straight at Jake, a furious scowl on his face.

"This guy says the doctor is trying to pin Amberleigh's murder on *him*," Jake said, pointing the gun at the scowling man.

"Why would Douglas have killed Amberleigh? They didn't even know each other."

"That's the part he's remaining a little too tight-lipped about," Jake said.

"I don't have to tell you anything. Either of you. Kill me if you want. I'm dead either way."

Zara wasn't sure what swept over her. A surge of fury so bright and potent it took over everything. Reason. Compassion. What was right and wrong. *Amberleigh* was dead. She didn't have a choice—hadn't had one, as far as Zara could tell.

Why did this guy get one? "I don't plan on killing you," she said, her grip on the gun so tight it hurt. She eyed the man, aimed her gun between his legs. "Just causing some damage."

She didn't miss the way Jake's eyebrows winged up—surprise, maybe even some discomfort. But he stood behind her. Backing her up.

"You shoot me, you'll either miss or kill me."

"That's funny, I didn't miss or kill you when I was back there. I'm *much* closer now." To prove it—and her impeccable aim—she shot at the grass, between his legs, without hitting anything. But close enough to scare the life out of him.

He scrambled back on a high-pitched scream. "Okay, okay," he said his voice quite a few octaves higher than it had been. He brought one hand to his ear, as if it was in pain.

Zara was so furious she barely noticed the dull echo of the very loud gunshot in her ears. "Tell me what happened. Now."

"Amberleigh was working the doctor over a little bit, and since she knew he'd been dating one of you, all she had to do was pretend to be her. He had some access to things we needed. So it worked out."

"Worked out?"

"Drugs," Jake said flatly. "Amberleigh was pretending to be Hazeleigh and conning the doctor out of drugs. Or prescriptions. So you could sell them, I assume?"

The man shrugged. "So what? How the hell else am I supposed to make a living around here?"

"Amberleigh…worked with you?" Zara said, because it still didn't fully make sense to her. "To get and sell the drugs?"

"You guys gonna turn me over to the cops or what?"

Zara looked over at Jake. She honestly didn't know how to sort through all of this.

"Seems like you'd have just as much reason to kill Amberleigh as the doctor."

"Are you kidding? Do you know how much money I made off of Amberleigh? Girl could talk a prescription pad or case of tranqs out of just about anyone. As far as I'm concerned, that doctor owes me now. That's why we're here. If you two hadn't started interfering."

"He owes you because my sister made you *money*?"

Zara didn't realize she'd aimed the gun again at first. She only saw red, only felt a well of grief and rage. But Jake's hand gently rested over hers on the gun.

"We should get out of here," he said in low tones.

"You can't leave me to his guys," the man yelled.

Jake shrugged and began to pull Zara away. He also pried her fingers off the gun and took it.

"Who taught you to shoot like that?" he murmured as they began to walk.

"No one. I just practiced. Jake…"

He shook his head as if in some kind of amazement. "I think I'm in love with you. Come on." He pulled her back into the dark and began to run. "We have to get out of here. We just walked into something far more complicated than we anticipated, and gunshots are going to lead to—" he stopped suddenly "—people coming. From both sides." He blew out a breath. "All right. Stick with me. Don't say a word."

He began to run again, her hand secure in his. She knew he was keeping his pace slower because of her, so she tried to increase her speed without being too loud. She let him lead her through the dark, because words like *love* were rattling around in her head along with more complications than they'd anticipated. Of course that love comment was a figure of speech…not…real.

They crested a snowy, rolling hill and there were lights in the distance. A house. The house.

Jake stopped her on a dime. He held her close. "I see two guards on the front. I think there are more. We've got a couple men behind us, but they're being more careful."

"So what do we do?"

"There's something due east. A fence or a…something. I can't quite make it out. But we're going to very slowly, very quietly move toward it. Hold my hand the whole way there, and if I give you a push, you run for it. No matter what. Got it?"

"Yeah." His hand slid down her arm to grasp her hand, fingers interlaced as he began to move. The pace was excruciatingly slow, but he was paying more attention to the house than their progress.

Rightfully so, if there were people closing in on them.

They reached whatever Jake had seen. A pillar of some kind that attached to a wrought iron fence. But the pillar was tall and thick and could hide both of them. Jake gave her hand a tug, pulling her into a squatting position against the brick.

"Can I have my phone back?"

She pulled it out of her pocket and handed it to him. He cursed quietly. "There's no service down here."

Zara thought about that text he'd asked her to send only if something went wrong. She leaned close to him, careful to keep her voice at a whisper. "I feel like I should tell you something."

"What's that?"

"I sent the SOS text to your brothers before you even got out of the car."

He was so still. Like, he didn't even take a breath.

But then he let out a long, slow exhale. "Well."

"I'm sorry."

"No, no, it's…fine. We're in a hell of a jam. If you couldn't get through to Thomas, they're the next best thing."

But he didn't sound certain about that. Of course, he didn't sound…upset either. Though it was hard to tell when they were speaking in hushed whispers. "You're not mad?"

"No, I think we're going to need the backup."

"Your…brothers."

"We were a military team. I'm not supposed to tell anyone that. No one is supposed to know anything about our past."

"Because…"

"Because we're terrorist targets if anyone ever finds us."

Terrorist targets. She blinked. "That sounds…bad." Which was a lame comment, but she didn't know what else to say to terrorist targets.

"Yeah, it does, doesn't it?" He sighed heavily. "Our histories, our identities were wiped so what was left of the terrorist organization we took down couldn't find us. We got new identities, a ranch in the middle of nowhere and presumably a place we could just disappear since the screwup was the military's fault."

Zara swallowed. She didn't know what to make of that. A terrorist target. Hiding in small-town Wyoming. She certainly believed he was the kind of man who'd taken out terrorist organizations, but to land here…

"So, it's all a lie. Jake Thompson is a lie?"

He made an odd noise. Not quite a sigh, not a grunt of pain. "Everything I've told you about my life is true, Zara. Foster care. Maybe I wasn't adopted into the guys' families, but we became each other's family. They are my brothers, and we all just want…to build a normal life. You can hate me for that. God knows, I'd get it."

"I don't hate you," Zara said quietly. She was still wrapping her brain around what he'd said. Here in the dark and cold. How could she hate him? "Why did you tell me?"

"I don't know. I shouldn't have. Cal will kill me if he ever finds out. We could be yanked if it ever got back to the man in charge of relocating us."

"Yanked. You mean…leave?"

"I'm not leaving. I'm not having another home ripped from me."

He said it with such vehemence, she believed him. And she believed him about the foster homes and the terrorist target no matter how crazy it all sounded, because he just… He made sense. Somehow. To her.

Except he was holding her hand. He'd said he *cared* about her and thought she was beautiful. So, she did the only thing she could think of.

She leaned her head on his shoulder and waited for the next step.

Chapter Twenty

Telling Zara what and who he was—no matter how few details—should have bothered Jake more than it did. But it was like a weight off his shoulders. When she leaned her head on his shoulder, it was like every step he'd ever taken in his life had led him right here.

Except he had to get them both out of this in one piece.

So, now his brothers-in-arms would show up, and if they got themselves too wrapped up in this, the boss would pull the plug. And Jake knew without a shadow of a doubt, he'd fight a reassignment. They wouldn't take him from this new life. They wouldn't take him from Zara.

But that'd be a lot easier to make happen if he could extract them all from this problem before the police got mixed up in it. Which meant he had to stop thinking about Zara and, worst of all, himself.

He needed to focus on the task at hand. "Do we believe that guy? That the doctor killed Amberleigh?"

"It makes sense… I guess. I don't know why Amberleigh would have been involved in drugs. Selling or getting or whatever. She ran away from home, sure, but she could have come home. We would have taken care of her."

Jake didn't say anything to that. He might not have had a real family, but some of his brothers had. And had purposefully left them behind—choosing possible death to having to go back and face them.

Sometimes going home was a lot more complicated than if people would take care of you or not.

But there was a second part to all this. Not just Amberleigh's murder, but someone trying to pin it on Hazeleigh. "Zara, would that doctor know you guys kept a key to your cabin under that plant on the porch?"

She was quiet for a moment, perhaps both surprised by the question but also considering. "I doubt it. We don't tell anyone about the key. He might have seen Hazeleigh use it, but then wouldn't he have used it when he was harassing Hazeleigh?"

"Are you so sure he didn't?" Jake asked gently. Because Zara hadn't noticed someone had been in her cabin before he had. Couldn't the doctor have been in there, messing with things the sisters didn't notice?

"He could have done it like that guy said, and he could be the one trying to pin it on Hazeleigh. It makes a twisted kind of sense, doesn't it?" Her hand shook in his—cold or adrenaline wearing off or just exhaustion. He pulled her close, for warmth, for comfort.

She leaned into him, so he adjusted them into a sitting position, leaning against the pillar. It gave them cover on one side and a line of sight on the other. Hard to sneak up on them this way. Now he just needed a way out of this.

He played over everything that had happened. "The

drug guy—his two men who came as backup had followed us from the hotel."

"So, they're part of the group that wanted to kidnap me?"

"Unless there's a third group. But if Amberleigh was impersonating Hazeleigh to get the drugs…maybe they wanted you to do the same."

"Like hell I would."

"I assume that's why they felt the need to kidnap."

Zara let out a long, shuddering breath. "Douglas killed Amberleigh. Because he thought she was Hazeleigh? Because he figured out what she was doing? I don't understand how someone could…could…"

"I've killed people, Zara."

She stiffened, but then she shook her head. "It's different. It's different when you're in the military."

"Maybe. And it never set…well. You convince yourself you're doing it for the good of other people not losing their lives, but it weighs on you. Or I should say, it weighs on some people. The point I'm trying to make is, killing doesn't bother some people. It makes them feel important or powerful. And the whys of that don't have anything to do with Amberleigh. They have everything to do with Douglas."

"I guess." She rested her head on his shoulder, her body leaning closer to his. She sighed again when he wrapped his arm around her shoulders.

"Not quite what I expected to find."

Jake had the presence of mind to clap his hand over Zara's mouth, muffling the scream of surprise she made at Cal's unexpected voice.

"It's just Cal," he murmured into her ear. She nodded against his hand, and he released her and got to his feet. "You made good time," Jake said. He ignored Cal's comment.

"Not going to lie, we were on our way the minute you said to wait for an SOS," Landon said.

Jake realized they must all be there, hidden in various shadows. Because if there was one thing Team Breaker knew how to do, it was disappear.

"Dunne's taking care of those guys you took out at the road." That came from Brody. "We loaded them into the truck and he'll dump them not far from the hospital. Then he'll come back and pick us up."

"Hopefully we're done by then," Cal continued. "What's the status?"

Jake didn't care for Cal's tone of voice. Disapproving and controlling. He didn't have time to fight Cal for the upper hand, and he needed Cal's help and expertise. So he just pretended he didn't feel the undercurrents. "We have two problems here," Jake said.

Zara stood, putting her hand on his back. A bodily move of support, as if she felt or heard the undercurrents, and was backing him over Cal.

He didn't have time for petty infighting, but he couldn't deny it felt good to have Zara supporting him.

"If the information we have is correct, the man who lives in this house is the one who killed Zara's sister. And might even be the one trying to frame Hazeleigh for the murder. But we've got another group out here. One Amberleigh was working for. From what we can tell, they want Zara so they can use her identical face in whatever scheme they had going with Amberleigh. On the positive side, they're also after the doctor."

"Sounds complicated," Landon offered.

"Those are just the parts we're aware of," Jake said, knowing it wouldn't particularly help his case with Cal. But still, they had to have eyes wide open going into this.

"This all sounds like a job for the police," Cal said in that I'm-the-leader voice that had worked in Syrian deserts and Iraqi hotspots but not so much here. Now. "We'll get you guys out, tow Jake's truck and leave it to them."

That wasn't going to work for Jake.

ZARA HELD HER BREATH. It was certainly an option. One that would keep them all out of trouble and danger—or at least bigger trouble.

"But…" She swallowed. She didn't feel right bringing all these guys into it. Guys who were apparently terrorist targets. But didn't that mean they could handle this? Didn't Jake sticking with her through this entire thing mean she should see it through to the end? "What if we call the police and they don't find anything to exonerate Hazeleigh? The police won't listen to the word of a drug dealer."

"You don't have to be here, Cal," Jake said, and his tone was *frigid*. It made Zara want to shiver. Instead, she pressed her hand to his back.

But he continued to speak to Cal. "We're not a team anymore. Feel free to head home," Jake said, a challenge laced with hurt, though Zara wondered if anyone noticed aside from her.

There was a long, tense silence.

"What's the plan?" one of the men who wasn't Cal

asked. She couldn't make them all out in the dark. She recognized Cal's weighty, authoritative voice and Landon's joking, ease-the-tension quips, but Brody and Henry sounded the same to her here in the dark.

"We have two objectives. First and foremost, keep Zara away from the group that wanted to kidnap her. There were two other men who arrived here before us. I don't know where they are or what they're doing, but they're here somewhere. They might be after the doctor in the moment, but they'd take her in a heartbeat."

"So we'll take Zara out," Cal said.

"No. You won't take me out." Maybe if she had nothing to offer, she could understand. But everything Jake had been talking about had given her an idea. "I have the same face. You might be able to use me. I could... convince Douglas that I'm Hazeleigh. Maybe. And then maybe he'd confess or something, and I could record it on my phone. Or... I don't know. Maybe there's a better plan, but you need to keep me around in case you can use me. I'll take the risk."

"No. You won't," Jake returned firmly. "We'll take the risks."

"I understand you know how to do this, that you have experience with...missions or whatever. I get it. But she's my sister. All these people around here, whoever they're with, whatever they're doing, they hurt my sisters in *some* way. I have to do everything I can to make sure they pay for that."

"She knows about missions," Cal muttered disgustedly.

Jake clearly ignored the comment. "We could use her," he said reluctantly. "But no taped confessions.

No…going in there trying to convince him you're Hazeleigh."

"The other group is ticked at the doctor too?" Brody or Henry asked.

"Yes. We could do an Op B," Jake returned.

"What's an Op B?" Zara asked.

But he didn't answer. Jake turned away from her and when he spoke, she realized it was at his brothers, leaving her completely out of it. Maybe not meaning to, but they'd changed into what she assumed was some kind of military mode and she couldn't follow all the acronyms and code words they seemed to be using.

But they hadn't sent her away. She held on to that.

"We stay at a distance. Pretend we have Hazeleigh. In the dark, far away, Zara won't have to really pretend. He'll just assume we have Hazeleigh."

"Even though Hazeleigh's in jail? If he's obsessed with her, surely he knows her whereabouts."

"Maybe, but I think we can fast talk our way around that." Jake turned to her in the dark. "You won't do anything or say anything. You're basically a prop. If things go sideways, your only objective is to—"

"Run," she finished for him. "And what would have happened if I had run the last time you told me to?"

"I would have been fine. It just would have…taken a little longer."

"Well, time is of the essence because you know Thomas also has someone looking for us now."

"Would it really be so bad if the police showed up?" Cal asked.

"Not…too bad. But there's a slight problem." Jake

explained the bloody necklace, and Zara winced as Cal swore harshly.

"Maybe we made a few miscalculations," Jake offered.

"Maybe?" Cal returned incredulously.

"But no one would even be looking at Douglas if we hadn't. So, sometimes miscalculations work out. You should know that better than anyone. And if we can prove Douglas had *something* to do with it, we can explain the necklace away and they will be more inclined to believe us rather than try Hazeleigh for murder."

"All right. Well, if you're taking the lead on this, organize the teams."

Even in the dark, Zara could tell Jake was a little taken aback by Cal's acquiescence of decision making. But he recovered quickly.

"Brody and Henry, you'll scout out the perimeter. We need a guard head count, an idea of the security measures on the—"

He stopped talking abruptly and then grabbed her fiercely. She had a sense there was some kind of communication going on between the men—though she couldn't hear or see anything.

Then there was a beam of light. It was pointed straight at Zara, and she winced and threw up her arms to shield her eyes from the painfully bright and surprising light.

Then she was being shoved. Hard. Her eyes flew open, but it was dark again and she couldn't see. The shove was hard enough she fell to the ground.

She lay there, not sure what to do in the dark with muffled grunts and thudding sounds of punches landing around her. The flashlight had fallen to the ground, so she could only see the occasional pair of boots come into view in that beam of light.

She began to inch toward it on her hands and knees, not wanting to draw any attention to herself. If she could get the flashlight, she could see what was going on. She could help.

Someone tripped over her and fell to the ground with a crash and a yelp of surprised pain, likely landing at an odd angle or hurting themselves trying to stop the fall. It didn't *sound* like one of Jake's brothers, but in the dark, she couldn't be sure.

She kept moving, got to within an arm's reach of the flashlight. She could see two men fighting to the side. She reached out to grab the flashlight, to try to hopefully point it more toward them so she could make out who was who, but right before she managed to get her fingers around the flashlight, someone pulled her roughly to her feet.

She was about to fight with everything she had, but she sagged with relief when she realized it was Jake. But he held her strangely. Not roughly, but with one arm around her midsection and in front of him, like he was holding her against her will, though he wasn't. Like he was using her as a shield when *that* would never happen.

"Sorry," he whispered, and then pressed the barrel of his gun to her temple.

"Come a step closer," Jake said, his voice loud and clear, and Zara realized he was speaking to someone else. "And your boss is going to be pretty mad at you."

A man all in black, now holding the flashlight in

one hand and a high-powered-looking gun in the other, was facing off with Jake. But Jake held her in front of him, the gun to her temple.

It was a very strange, uncomfortable feeling, but he kept his hold on her gentle, and while that steadied her some, she knew it didn't look great to the security guard that had to believe this was Hazeleigh.

The security guard studied Jake in the flashlight beam. "Let's everyone just stay calm," the guard said carefully.

"Get your boss out here. *Now*," Jake returned, his voice gravelly and cold. "He has five minutes."

Chapter Twenty-One

Jake had been in a lot of terrible situations but few matched having to hold a gun to Zara's head and pretend like he might kill her. Knowing he had to make it realistic.

Luckily, the guard seemed to believe him. He'd backed slowly away, toward the house.

His brothers had scattered after taking care of the other two guards who had snuck up on them. Jake still wasn't sure if they were the doctor's guards or members of the other guy's little drug gang, but it didn't matter. They'd taken care of them.

Now they needed the doctor.

Maybe the plan hadn't been fully fleshed out, but Jake trusted each of his brothers to do what was right. Necessary.

For the briefest moment, he rested his cheek against the top of Zara's head. He didn't dare put the gun down. He wasn't sure he'd be able to bring it back up, and here in the dark, it was too easy to be caught off guard.

"You need to take my hair down," Zara whispered.

"Huh?"

"My hair should be down. I'll look more like Hazeleigh if my hair is down. If I can have five seconds to take the coat off and tie it around my waist—"

"It's freezing out here."

"That'll add to it. Me shivering and uncomfortable. Hazeleigh isn't big on jeans, but it'll be more like her if I have the coat tied around my waist. Hair down. Just pull the band out and undo the braid."

She was likely right. She'd certainly know better than him. It worried him, the time it would take, but he didn't have time to waver then. "Okay. Quickly. Take off the coat and I'll handle the hair."

She shrugged out of the coat, and he pulled the band out of the braid while she tied the coat around her waist. Her hair stayed wound together so he had to quickly unravel the twisted strands while still holding the gun close enough to her head it didn't look like he was about to let her go.

Light flooded on from the house. Jake forced himself not to flinch or close his eyes in instinctual response.

They were now swathed in it. The whole front yard practically bright as day. It wouldn't help them with pretending Zara was Hazeleigh, but for now, they had to stick with the plan. Jake looked around quickly. He saw two men lying on the ground—neither were Jake's brothers, so they had to be either more security for the doctor or the group that wanted drugs.

The guard from before stepped back out of the house, followed by a tall man with sandy-blond hair.

"I suppose for a couple of thugs, you think this is very impressive."

"You must be Douglas Nichols."

"Dr. Nichols," the man corrected. "It'll do well for you to remember I'm a *doctor*, with unlimited connections and resources. Whatever your sad little group is trying to do will only get you in trouble. The police *are* on their way."

"Are they?" Jake returned, as if he was unbothered, though the police being on their way definitely put a wrench in his plans. Maybe they'd look closer at Douglas because of this, but maybe they'd find that bloody necklace in his truck and draw all the wrong conclusions. "Then we better hurry this up. You'll be taking the blame for Amberleigh Hart's murder or you'll have another murder on your doorstep that I'll make sure the police take a real hard look at you for, *Doctor*."

The man scoffed.

"I don't know why you think I'd care what a careless group of drug-addicted criminals would do to that woman."

Jake had a beat to think, to pivot. He looked at Zara in disgust. "I thought you told me he cared about you."

"I… He did. I thought he did. Maybe Zara was right."

Jake was impressed by how different Zara managed to sound. Uncertain and stuttering, as though she was both afraid and another person entirely. The skittish Hazeleigh.

"Hazeleigh is in jail," Douglas said flatly. "I'm not a moron."

"Zara took my spot," Zara blurted.

The doctor blinked at that, and Jake had to fight to keep his own surprise out of his expression.

"When they were coming to arrest me," Zara continued, still speaking in that breathier, more halting pattern of speech. "We switched places. She didn't think I'd make it in jail. You know how protective she is."

"You've been…pretending to be Zara," the doctor said, clearly trying to sound like he didn't believe her, but there was enough speculation in his gaze it was obvious he wasn't convinced one way or another.

Zara nodded. "I've done all her chores. Gone to visit Zara in jail. One of those men who bought our ranch was even helping me look for who killed Amberleigh, thinking I was Zara. Zara's really the only one who knows me well enough to tell. Well, and you, of course."

Jake had to angle himself so his face was hidden behind Zara's head because he wanted to laugh. She was laying it on a little thick, but the doctor seemed to be eating it up, and that's all that mattered.

"Come here."

Zara stepped forward, but Jake's grip tightened, and though it pained him, he jabbed the gun tighter against her temple. "Uh-uh. You give me what I want first," Jake said, shifting so he could glare at the doctor again.

Douglas sighed heavily. Dramatically. "What you really want are drugs. The woman currently in jail will take the fall for the murder. That doesn't matter any. We'll set that aside." He said it without pause. Just a man issuing orders, like Jake would automatically follow.

"I know your little friend was more interested in the prescriptions, but that's simply far too easy to trace back to me, which I tried to tell her. It's really her own fault she wouldn't just listen."

"You killed her because she wouldn't listen?"

"I killed her because she was a duplicitous, argumentative, piece of trash who thought she was better than me and my beloved." He said all of that with a pleasant smile, but his hand had curled into a fist. "Now, let Hazeleigh go and we'll come to some sort of deal. The police *are* on their way, so time is wasting."

"Let me go," Zara said under her breath.

"Over my dead body," Jake muttered right back.

"We're going to hide," Jake said firmly to Douglas. "You're going to get rid of the cops. *Then* we can talk."

"You will not be issuing orders. Now. Men?" Douglas snapped his fingers and the man next to him used some kind of two-way com unit. But all the response was static.

Then Cal, Brody and Landon stepped into the light.

"Sorry, buddy," Landon said with a grin. "I think we took care of your *men*."

ZARA THOUGHT SHE should feel some kind of relief. Surely Jake and his brothers could take care of a doctor and one security guard. And Douglas had confessed. Out loud. In front of all of them.

But the tension inside of her only wound tighter. Because while Jake's brothers had moved into the light, Jake hadn't moved. He didn't put the gun down. They were still playing a game, and as long as they were playing it, everyone was in danger.

The guard with Douglas had a gun. Zara couldn't tell if it was pointed at any of the brothers in particular or if he was just ready to shoot at wherever the threat came from.

Each of Jake's brothers had a gun—most looked like the guns Jake had picked off the drug dealer before the brothers had arrived.

"Face it, Doc," Jake said. "You're surrounded. You've confessed to murder. Have your man put down his weapon. Maybe we'll wait for the cops after all."

"Oh yes. The police will believe a band of drug-dealing thugs who held Hazeleigh Hart at gunpoint over an upstanding doctor with a spotless reputation," Douglas said, disdain and condescension dripping from every word. "You can't beat me. I thought of every possibility. There is no way anyone can pin Amberleigh's murder on me."

"That a fact?" Jake returned. "Anybody get it?"

Cal held up a phone, and though it was tinny and far away and she could only hear muffled words, she realized it was video. Video of Douglas admitting to the murder without any provocation.

Zara looked away from the video to Douglas. She wanted to see the realization dawn on him that he'd been caught. That he'd done it to himself.

But she saw something grim and dangerous in his expression. Like when he'd been outside their cabin and she'd threatened to call the cops. He hadn't hurt them. He'd just pounded on the door and demanded to see Hazeleigh, and Zara had determined he was harmless.

But he'd killed Amberleigh, so that couldn't be. She looked down at his hand and realized he was slowly pulling something from behind his back. There was only one thing it could be.

"Gun. Gun! He's got a—"

Jake practically threw her to the ground at just about

the same time a shot exploded around them. The fall to the ground jarred her, and it took a moment to regain her wits and get back up. She whirled around to where Douglas had been.

Henry held him now. The doctor struggled against him, but it was no use. Henry was bigger, stronger. Brody had the guard. Zara whirled to see if Cal had been hit.

But Cal was standing, still holding the phone out like he was showing it to everyone. There was a frozen look of pure, undiluted shock slackening his features.

Because Jake was crumpled on the ground in front of him.

Zara's heart simply stopped. "No." She lurched toward him, and by the time she got there, Cal had gathered his wits enough to be kneeling next to him, rolling him over.

Zara barely heard the sound of anguish that came out of her own mouth. He'd been shot. Cal immediately put his hands over the bleeding wound on Jake's stomach.

"No, no, no." Zara fell to the ground next to him. She touched his face. "Jake."

"I'll be fine," he muttered, but his eyes were closed and his words were slurred and *pain* radiated from him.

But he was alive. Talking. Writhing in pain. "Jake…" She didn't know what to say or do. "Please."

Someone tried to nudge her out of the way, but she slapped at them. She couldn't leave him. She couldn't… "Jake. Jake." She didn't know what to say. She wanted to demand he open his eyes. Demand he be fine. Yell at him for being a jackass. *A hero.*

"Zara, get out of the way. Dunne can help, but you need to move. You have to give him room to work."

It took a few more seconds for the words—Cal's words—to actually penetrate her brain. She stopped fighting the arms that pulled her away, as she realized Dunne was in fact there, already pressing something to that awful bleeding hole in Jake's abdomen. He had a bag or something. Medical supplies. He was going to make it okay. He *had* to make it okay.

Cal was the one who had dragged her away.

"It's going to be alright," Cal said roughly. "Dunne has experience with this."

Because they'd each been hurt before. To war before. Together. A team. *Brothers*.

But Jake had moved to save Cal. To take the bullet instead.

"I can hold his hand. I can talk to him. I can—"

"Just give Dunne room to work."

She whirled at Cal as a tide of anger and fear swept up and over any last vestiges of reason. "Why'd you let him do it?" she demanded, tears pouring down her face no matter how she tried to restrain them. She pushed at Cal. "You shouldn't have let him jump in front of you."

Cal didn't say anything. He stood there with that same frozen shock on his face as from before.

Zara couldn't stand to look at him any longer. As far as she was concerned, this was half his fault.

But only half. She looked around the yard and found the other half. She stormed over to where Henry held a still-struggling Douglas. She marched right up to him, the need to hurt him so very potent she didn't even question it.

"You're not Hazeleigh," he said with disgust as she approached. "You lying—"

She punched him. Hard as she could, right in the throat where she knew it would do a decent amount of painful damage.

"You will rot in jail and hell for what you did to my sisters and Jake."

She could tell he wanted to respond, but he was still too busy gasping for air. She wanted to punch him again. Take one of the guns from Henry or Brody and shoot him. Kill him like he'd killed Amberleigh.

But she only stood there as the red haze of fury and fear began to drain out of her, into a numbness.

That's when she heard the sirens. Sirens. Help. God, they needed help. She started to run toward them. Cal did too, and beat her to where an ambulance had parked behind two Bent County Sheriff's Department cruisers.

"He's been shot," Cal was saying as he led an EMT over to where Dunne was still working on Jake.

Jake, still as death. She moved for him again, but someone grabbed her arm. She whirled, ready to punch and fight her way out of whoever's grasp. But it was Thomas. Still not in uniform.

She dropped her bunched fist. She couldn't read his expression. "Let me go."

"Give them room to work," he said flatly.

Why was everyone telling her to give them room? Jake needed someone. Someone to hold his hand. Someone to tell him… She didn't know, but she couldn't stand this. "I need to be with him."

"I'll drive you to the hospital."

"But you have work here."

He shook his head. "I can't be on this case, Zara. I'm only here because of you." He tugged her arm. She wanted to shake it off, but they were moving Jake onto a stretcher. The low murmurings were nonsense to her. She didn't know any medical terms.

Dunne moved with the EMTs, talking to them in serious tones. And he got into the ambulance as they loaded the stretcher, so Jake wasn't alone. He was with his brother.

Thomas pulled her arm again. "Come on. We'll follow."

So she walked with him to his car. His personal car because he wasn't acting as sheriff's deputy here. He was here as her cousin. He'd come because…

Well, likely because she'd lied to him. In a way that might get him in trouble with his job. She closed her eyes, too many emotions battling for prominence, so she just felt like she'd hit a brick wall. Impenetrable. Heavy.

"You lied to me," he said after a long while of following the ambulance, his eyes on the road ahead of them.

"Yes," she said and felt guilty despite herself. "Now we know who killed Amberleigh. You're welcome." And Jake had been shot trying to save his brother. His brother who had only been there because Zara had gotten Jake all mixed up in this.

She'd figured he was something like invincible. He could fight men off with weapons and pretend to hold a gun to her head. He could help her—when no one else in her life had ever really helped. Ever really just *been* there.

But he couldn't let his brother get shot.

She closed her eyes against the wave of pain. When the car stopped, she opened her eyes and saw the hospital entrance. She didn't know what she felt. She didn't know how to *bear* any of this. But she wanted to do it alone.

Alone was what she should have been all along. "I don't need you to come in with me."

Thomas looked at her, a mix of hurt and something else in his gaze. He shook his head. "Maybe you don't, Zaraleigh, but it's about time people stopped listening to what you say you don't need."

In a different moment, she might have been offended enough to yell at him, but he parked the car and took her by the arm as though she wasn't strong enough to walk on her own.

She swallowed at the lump in her throat and had to admit to herself that Thomas knew where to go a lot better than she did. He took her to a waiting room where Jake's brothers were sitting or standing in various positions.

"Any news?" she asked. Any of them. All of them.

Cal shook his head. He was staring at his hands. Clearly he'd been cleaned up a little bit, but there were still traces of blood there.

Jake's blood.

It hurt, but something about the way Thomas was still holding her arm reminded her that hurt wasn't all about anger. Anger was easier, certainly. A safer place to hurt, but it wasn't…right.

"I need to apologize for what I said to you back there," she managed to say to Cal.

He laughed, bitterly, and shook his head. "Why?"

"It's not your fault he jumped in front of you. He would have jumped in front of anyone. That's…who he is." The lump in her throat seemed insurmountable, but she forced the words out. "He saves people."

That didn't seem to ease the guilt Cal clearly held on his own shoulders, but he feigned a smile anyway. "You're right about that."

A nurse bustled in and surveyed the group. "Are any of you Jake Thompson's immediate family?"

Cal stood, and all the other brothers waited. Because Cal was their leader, even in this. "I'm his brother."

"All right. Come with me."

Cal followed the nurse.

And Zara could only wait.

Chapter Twenty-Two

Zara was numb. No one at the hospital would tell her anything, and Cal didn't come back before Laurel showed up and pulled her aside.

"We're going to need a formal statement. Dr. Nichols already has lawyers crawling all over the station, so the sooner we do this the better."

Lawyers. "But he did it. He admitted to doing it on video."

"Yes, and Mr. Thompson handed his phone over to the police officers at the scene, but we still need to make this case airtight. I want a statement from you, but let's find somewhere a little private."

Laurel took her arm like Thomas had.

"I'll text you if there are any updates," Thomas said. Even though he didn't need to stay. He didn't *need* to do any of this. He was doing it because they were family.

Zara felt shamed for lying to him, even knowing they'd had to do it. Shamed that she hadn't leaned on him in the beginning of all this when maybe she should have trusted him.

Too late now.

Laurel led her out of the waiting room and into the

main lobby of the hospital. She found a bench in a little alcove. They sat down, practically hip to hip.

"We'll start back at the hotel. I want you to tell me everything from there until Thomas drove you to the hospital. No detail is too small."

Zara swallowed and nodded. It felt like so much pressure, and instead of Jake sitting next to her, holding her hand, she was alone. He was in an ICU room…

Getting help. He was getting *help*. She had to remind herself of that.

She took a deep breath and tried to remember everything. Arriving at the hotel. Their plan. Zara recounted it all, but when she got to Thomas showing up… "I don't want Thomas to get into any trouble. He was trying to do the right thing, really. We lied to him and—"

"It's imperative you tell me the whole truth, Zara, but I have a confession to make that might make you feel better about Thomas keeping some things from me." Laurel shifted on the bench. "I saw you. You and Jake in the hallway at the hotel. Kissing."

Zara's mouth dropped. "What?"

"It was a valiant effort to hide in plain sight, but I'm a detective. I pay attention to details. What boots a person wears, the way they hold themselves when they're trying to hide something. And a million other things that made you two instantly recognizable."

"But you didn't…" Zara tried to work through it. Laurel had recognized them, but she hadn't stopped them. "You let us go."

"Yes, I did."

"Why?"

"Because…I believe in law and order. I believe in

investigating by the book because I have to build a case. I have to make sure the right outcome follows solving a crime. But I also know what it's like to have the law be in your way. To need to go around it to keep the people you love safe, or find the truth. I wasn't about to stop you from finding that."

Zara didn't know what to say.

"So, no. Thomas won't be in trouble for not telling us he'd found you guys."

"Detective… Laurel… He killed her. Douglas *killed* Amberleigh. He can't get away with it."

Laurel reached out and patted Zara's hand. "We will do everything in our power to make sure he doesn't. The fact of the matter is, I don't believe in a perfect crime. I believe we would have figured this out…eventually. But it would have taken a long time. Dr. Nichols definitely covered his tracks, and you and Jake interfering the way you did allowed us to connect him to everything a lot quicker than we would have, and the video confession tightens the case considerably. I can't say you did the *right* thing, because you could have let Thomas and me in on some of this, but you didn't do the *wrong* thing either. Now, tell me the rest."

Zara went through all of it, only choking up when she got to the part where Jake had been shot. Shot protecting his brother.

Laurel's hand patted hers again, and this time stayed on top. "I know it's hard watching someone you love get hurt. I've been through that a time or two myself, or been the one getting hurt. You've been through a lot of hurts. It's okay to…let yourself feel all that. No one expects you to power through losing your sister and watching your boyfriend get shot."

Love. Boyfriend. They'd kissed. Once. For fake reasons. And yet…*love* felt exactly right. But there were more people she loved involved in this.

"My sister?"

"Hazeleigh is in the process of being released. She's having a friend pick her up since you're otherwise detained." Noting Zara's discomfort, she looked through her notes. "Friend's name is Kate Phillips?"

Zara nodded. Kate would be good for Hazeleigh. Calm and good at taking care. Something Zara wasn't good at.

Laurel asked a few more questions, noted everything down. Recorded some things. Zara was exhausted by the time Laurel was satisfied, and she hadn't realized she'd dozed off until her phone buzzed.

She jolted awake and looked up. Instead of Laurel sitting on the bench with her, it was Thomas.

"Laurel thought it best to let you sleep."

Zara nodded, then her phone buzzed again and she pawed at her pocket. She opened the text message from Cal.

Awake. Okay. I'll sneak you in.

Zara hopped to her feet. "Cal said he can sneak me in."

Thomas took her arm as she began to walk back to the waiting room. She frowned at him. "I can walk, you know."

"You can walk, sure. You can lean too."

She stared at him a long time. "I'm sorry. That we lied to you. I really am. I just thought it was the only way."

"I'm sorry you thought it was the only way, Zara."

Zara didn't know what to say to that, so she decided she'd go ahead and get better at leaning, and she let Thomas hold on to her while they walked back to the waiting room.

WHEN JAKE WOKE UP, groggy and fuzzy-headed, he thought he was back in a military hospital in the Middle East. Cal was here, after all, looking guilty and furious at once.

But he wasn't in his military uniform or even his civilian, desert clothes. He was dressed in ranch clothes. Because they were in Wyoming.

"Zara." His voice came out a croak with no real enunciation, but Cal seemed to understand.

"She's on her way."

Jake let out a breath and relaxed into the bed. He managed to swallow some of the rustiness in his voice away. "Going to live then, I guess?"

"Looks like. Going to have to take it easy for a while. Clean shot and all, but it'll take a while to heal."

Cal didn't give anything away in his voice, but Jake knew it wouldn't set well with him that Jake had risked his life over him. "Had to do it, you know."

"You really didn't."

"I was the only reason you were there. You couldn't go down because you'd taken the video. Because I needed your help."

"Would have preferred it."

Jake let out a little laugh, but even with the drug haze, he could feel the pain. "You need your head examined, Cal."

"Maybe."

They lapsed into a silence, but it had weight.

"Let me guess," Jake offered. "The boss wants to pull us."

Cal said nothing but eventually nodded.

Jake shook his head. "I'm not going. I'm not. They can't force me. It was their screwup that led us here. I'm not losing this." *I'm not losing her.*

"That's what I told him."

Jake had been ready to rail at Cal, but that stopped him. "What?"

"What? I watched Zara—Zara Hart, who I saw get kicked in the shoulder by one of the cows and not cry— sob all over your sorry ass. Then take a chunk out of me because she was so upset that you'd been hurt. She was *inconsolable.* I don't know anything about love, but I suppose if it's real, that's it."

Jake shifted uncomfortably. *Love.* It was a big, scary word that kept cropping up.

"So, I told the boss that you'd done more for our case by helping a local girl than us pretending to be six related loners could. That you were the one who thought we should get involved so people take us at face value and ask fewer questions. I told him it worked. You'd be hailed a hero, and people would stop looking into our backgrounds."

"I can't imagine he took that very well."

"Not at first, but when I told him you had a local girlfriend, he warmed to the idea."

"Huh?"

"Oh, he said getting married to a local was a great idea. Connects you to the community, lends credibility to our backstory. He was all for it."

"Married?" Jake practically squeaked.

Cal chuckled. "Well, you're well enough to know that's a terrifying thought, but we're staying put, Jake. I'll fight the boss on that. I promise you that."

"I don't need your penance, Cal."

"Maybe not, but you've got it."

Something caught both their attention, and they looked over at the door. Zara was standing there.

"Sorry to interrupt. Dunne showed me the way."

Cal shook his head. "No interruption. I'll wait outside." And he was gone in mere seconds.

Leaving Zara and Jake alone. Her hair was a mess, her clothes still wet and dirty from all the running around in the snow. But she was whole and in one piece and *beautiful*.

"You're okay," she said in a squeaky voice he could hardly reconcile with the Zara he knew.

"I told you I was."

She smiled faintly, finally moving across the room. She looked down at him, brushed her fingers across his forehead. "You're an idiot," she said, tears in her eyes.

"Yeah." He reached up and found her hand with his. "Going to have to get used to my idiocy."

Something flickered in her eyes that had Jake realizing she might have heard… "I don't know how much you heard of what Cal said, but—"

"We should probably go on a few dates before we

decide if we want to get married," she said seriously, but there was mischief in his eyes.

Jake laughed. Winced. Sighed. "Come here." He gave her arm a little tug.

She looked a little uncertain, but with extraordinary care, she slid into the bed next to him, still holding his hand and managing to avoid all the machines hooked up to him. She rested her head on his shoulder.

And everything inside of him eased. He lifted his hand, drew it down her tangled mess of hair. Despite the gunshot-wound discomfort and his exhaustion, something right washed over him. Exactly right.

Her. Here. Them.

"How's Hazeleigh?"

She sighed. "She went home with Kate. I'll have to go to her, but I needed to see you first." She rested her hand on his chest, gingerly. "Are you sure you're okay?"

"Going to be a bit of a healing process, but I've survived worse." Which reminded him that he'd…told her. Everything. "Listen, about what I told you back there…"

She lifted her head so she could look him in the eye. "I won't tell anyone. Ever," she said so seriously. A vow. "You're just Jake Thompson from…"

She knew his secret and would keep it. He knew she'd keep it, no matter what. So there was only the truth. "Pittsburgh."

She seemed to think this over. "A long way from Wyoming."

"Yeah, just a nomad looking for somewhere to belong."

Her brown eyes were suspiciously shiny, but no tears fell. "You belong here, Jake. That I'm certain of."

So was he, but that didn't mean things were easy. "Your land, your ranch. You love—"

"I do," she said, cutting him off. "I can't say I'm joyful about not owning Hart land, but the fact it's keeping you and your brothers safe? That's worth it to me."

Which didn't sit right at all. "You shouldn't always be the one taking care of everyone."

She studied his face, and it was like she understood him down to his soul. She knew his secrets. The things he didn't talk about. Somehow, she understood him. All of him, when he was certain no one would—or could—after all he'd been through.

"Some people take care," she said softly. She pointed to where he'd been shot. "Some people save. It's not so different really. And not as much of a sacrifice when you're doing what's right. For people you care about."

He didn't speak at first. He couldn't. Something had banded around his lungs, tight and squeezing. A depth of emotion he'd need more time to sort through, but there was a basic truth to *all* of this.

"I don't need a few dates to know that what I feel for you is big. Important. And that I don't want to let you go."

She studied him. Dark eyes so serious. Then, very carefully, she pressed her mouth to his. She sighed against his mouth. "I think that's a good place to start," she murmured.

Then she laid her head on his shoulder, hand on his chest.

A very good place to start.

Epilogue

When Zara got home, it was practically midafternoon, even though it felt like it should be the middle of the night. Thomas dropped her off and offered to stay with her, but she sent him on his way so she could be alone.

She had talked to Hazeleigh briefly on the phone, and her sister seemed content to stay at Kate's. Zara knew she should want to see her sister. Maybe even go over to Kate's and confront her. They had so much to talk about, but Zara needed…time. Strength.

She had to be strong for Hazeleigh and she just didn't feel very strong. So, she let the days stretch out. She talked to Jake on the phone, visited once the hospital allowed nonfamily, texted her sister, did ranch chores with the stoic Thompson brothers. On Christmas Eve, she went to her aunt and uncle's house in Bent, visited briefly with her father.

She'd taken Jake a Christmas Eve dinner, and he'd joked it was their first date when they ate it together in his hospital room.

Hazeleigh kept her distance.

So when Christmas dawned, bright and snowy, Zara decided enough was enough. She got up and dressed, determined to drive out to Kate's, even if it was too early, and demand to see Hazeleigh.

But when she stepped into the living room, the tree was glowing, even though she'd had the lights unplugged for days. Hazeleigh was sitting at the foot of the tree, looking at the lights. Until she turned her face to Zara.

She managed a small smile. "Merry Christmas."

Zara knew she should demand to know…a million things, but instead, when Hazeleigh got to her feet, she simply crossed the room and hugged her sister. They held on to each other for a long time.

"I'm sorry I stayed away," Hazeleigh said after a while, her voice squeaky. "I just…couldn't face it all. I couldn't come here knowing Douglas had been in there. Planting evidence against me." She shuddered. "A murderer."

"He's in jail now. I talked to Laurel yesterday and she's very pleased with the way the evidence is shaping up."

Hazeleigh nodded and tried to smile, but Zara knew it was fake. And because she did, she couldn't help herself from stepping back. From asking what she promised herself she wouldn't. "Why didn't you tell me? About Amberleigh being back?"

Hazeleigh sighed, then collapsed onto the couch. "I couldn't face you either. Because… Oh, Zara. I knew Amber was mixed up in some bad things. Right from the get-go. She was… I just knew she was lying to me. But I thought if I didn't tell you, if I tried to help her on my own, I might be able to get through to her. You two would have just fought, but I thought I could…fix it."

Zara was quiet. She didn't know what to say to that. It was the truth, but it still hurt because Hazeleigh had never lied to her before.

"I thought it was the group she was with. She told me how dangerous they were. How they'd killed some dealer of theirs who hadn't held up their end of the bargain. She was… She liked it, though, Zee. I couldn't believe it then. Didn't want to. But she liked doing bad things. She didn't deserve Douglas…"

Zara reached out—something she wasn't sure she would have been able to do if Jake hadn't shown her how easy it could be. She closed her hand over Hazeleigh's. "Don't blame yourself."

Hazeleigh looked down at their joined hands. A tear slid down her cheek. "She died pretending to be me."

"Yes, but that wasn't your choice. And it wasn't your choice to have Douglas be a murderer. You were the pawn, Haze. Not the cause." She grabbed her by the chin so Hazeleigh had to look her in the eye. "It's not your fault."

"Maybe not, but I feel like I'm always the pawn. I'm tired of it."

Zara didn't know what to say. It didn't seem right to tell Hazeleigh it was her choice what to be—pawn or in charge of her own life. So she simply sat in silence and held her sister's hand.

They both sighed at the same time and leaned their heads together, still holding hands. They'd lost the other piece of themselves, but they still had each other.

"I love you, Hazeleigh."

"I love you too."

They were quiet a long time, sitting on the couch, looking at the tree.

"How's Jake?" Hazeleigh asked after a long while.

"Healing well. He should be home tomorrow." Tomorrow. Today was Christmas, but Jake wouldn't be celebrating it in the hospital. She thought of the house, devoid of all Christmas decorations, and how much joy Hazeleigh always got out of decorating.

"I have an idea." She got to her feet and grinned at Hazeleigh. "How about we go be Christmas elves?"

"You *hate* Christmas decorating."

"No, I hate Christmas putting away. There's a difference. Come on." She grabbed Hazeleigh's arm.

A few hours later, after what Zara figured *might* constitute breaking and entering, the house they'd grown up in glowed with Christmas magic.

She stepped back to admire her handiwork. Then looked at her sister.

Hazeleigh was grinning. Color was back in her cheeks. Yeah, this had been a good idea. Even if the guys didn't appreciate it, Hazeleigh did.

"We should get going if we want to be gone before they get back," Zara said. The sun was setting, and the guys should be coming back in from the field soon. Someone would be at the hospital, but they had been taking turns staying with Jake during visitor hours. But Jake had told her not to come today, to spend Christmas with Hazeleigh and any other family she wanted to see.

She hadn't argued, but now she thought…she'd head out to the hospital anyway. Because who she really wanted to see was him. But before she could articulate any of that, the door opened.

Well, she'd face the brothers first, she supposed.

"Merry Christ…" She trailed off as Hazeleigh finished because, while four of the brothers had stepped inside, she was shocked to see Jake was standing in the center of them.

"Well, you two have been busy," Landon said with a grin. "Did you break into our house?"

But Zara barely heard him. Jake was *here*.

"They let me go a little early," he said, as if he too wasn't paying attention to anyone but her.

He was on two feet, standing on his own, and she hadn't realized until this moment how much worry she'd still been carrying about his recovery. But him being home…

She crossed the room and threw her arms around him. His came around hers. She was careful not to squeeze, not wanting to hurt him. But… "You're home," she whispered into his shoulder.

"Yeah, I am."

* * * * *

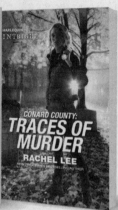

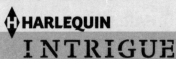

COMING NEXT MONTH FROM

INTRIGUE

#2103 CONARD COUNTY: CHRISTMAS CRIME SPREE
Conard County: The Next Generation • by Rachel Lee
Savage attacks on several women in parson Molly Canton's parish threaten the holiday season. Assisting Detective Callum McCloud's investigation, Molly is drawn to the tortured man. But once the detective realizes these attacks are a smoke screen obscuring the real target—Molly—the stakes escalate...especially now that Molly's goodness has breached Callum's calloused heart.

#2104 POLICE DOG PROCEDURAL
K-9s on Patrol • by Lena Diaz
When police lieutenant Macon Ridley and his K-9, Bogie, respond to a call from Daniels Canine Academy, they discover a baby on DCA's doorstep. Even more surprising, the chemistry that sizzled when Macon first met Emma Daniels sparks once again. Now, not only is an innocent infant's life at stake but so is Emma's...

#2105 EAGLE MOUNTAIN CLIFFHANGER
Eagle Mountain Search and Rescue • by Cindi Myers
Responding to the reports of a car accident, newcomer Deputy Jake Gwynn finds a murder scene instead. Search and rescue paramedic Hannah Richards tried to care for the likely suspect before he slipped away—and now he's gone from injured man to serial killer on the loose. And she's his next target.

#2106 SMALL TOWN VANISHING
Covert Cowboy Soldiers • by Nicole Helm
Rancher Brody Thompson's got a knack for finding things, even in the wild and remote Wyoming landscape he's just begun to call home. So when Kate Phillips asks for Brody's help in solving her father's decade-old disappearance, he's intrigued. But there's a steep price to pay for uncovering the truth...

#2107 PRESUMED DEAD
Defenders of Battle Mountain • by Nichole Severn
Forced to partner up, reserve officer Kendric Hudson and missing persons agent Campbell Dwyer work a baffling abduction case that gets more dangerous with each new revelation. As they battle a mounting threat, they must also trust one another with their deepest secrets.

#2108 WYOMING WINTER RESCUE
Cowboy State Lawmen • by Juno Rushdan
Trying to stop a murderous patient has consumed psychotherapist Lynn Delgado. But when a serial killer targets Lynn, she must accept protection and turn to lawman Nash Garner for help. As she flees the killer in a raging blizzard, Nash follows, risking everything to save the woman he's falling for.

HICNM0922

The whole desperate plan began simply as a last-ditch attempt to save his life. He never intended for anyone to get hurt. That day, not long after Thanksgiving, he walked into the bank full of hope. It was the first time he'd ever asked for a loan. It was also the first time he'd ever seen executive loan officer Carla Richmond.

When he tapped at her open doorway, she looked up from that big desk of hers. He thought she was too young and pretty with her big blue eyes and all that curly chestnut-brown hair to make the decision as to whether he lived or died.

She had a great smile as she got to her feet to offer him a seat.

He felt so out of place in her plush office that he stood in the doorway nervously kneading the brim of his worn baseball cap for a moment before stepping in. As he did, her blue-eyed gaze took in his ill-fitting clothing hanging on his rangy body, his bad haircut, his large, weathered hands.

He told himself that she'd already made up her mind before he even sat down. She didn't give men like him a second look—let alone money. Like his father always said, bankers never gave dough to poor people who actually needed it. They just helped their rich friends.

Right away Carla Richmond made him feel small with her questions about his employment record, what he had for collateral, why he needed the money and how he planned to repay it. He'd recently lost one crappy job and was in the process of starting another temporary one, and all he had to show for the years he'd worked hard labor since high school was an old pickup and a pile of bills.

He took the forms she handed him and thanked her, knowing he wasn't going to bother filling them in. On the way out of her office, he balled them up and dropped them in the trash. All the way to his pickup, he mentally kicked himself for being such a fool. What had he expected?

No one was going to give him money, even to save his life—especially some woman in a suit behind a big desk in an air-conditioned office. It didn't matter that she didn't have a clue how desperate he really was. All she'd seen when she'd looked at him was a loser. To think that he'd bought a new pair of jeans with the last of his cash and borrowed a too-large button-up shirt from a former coworker for this meeting.

After climbing into his truck, he sat for a moment, too scared and sick at heart to start the engine. The worst part was the thought of going home and telling Jesse. The way his luck was going, she would walk out on him. Not that he could blame her, since his gambling had gotten them into this mess.

He thought about blowing off work, since his new job was only temporary anyway, and going straight to the bar. Then he reminded himself that he'd spent the last of his money on the jeans. He couldn't even afford a beer. His own fault, he reminded himself. He'd only made things worse when he'd gone to a loan shark for cash and then stupidly gambled the money, thinking he could make back what he owed and then some when he won. He'd been so sure his luck had changed for the better when he'd met Jesse.

Last time the two thugs had come to collect the interest on the loan, they'd left him bleeding in the dirt outside his rented house. They would be back any day.

With a curse, he started the pickup. A cloud of exhaust blew out the back as he headed home to face Jesse with the bad news. Asking for a loan had been a long shot, but still he couldn't help thinking about the disappointment he'd see in her eyes when he told her. They'd planned to go out tonight for an expensive dinner with the loan money to celebrate.

As he drove home, his humiliation began to fester like a sore that just wouldn't heal. Had he known even then how this was going to end? Or was he still telling himself he was just a nice guy who'd made some mistakes, had some bad luck and gotten involved with the wrong people?

Don't miss
Christmas Ransom *by B.J. Daniels,*
available December 2022 wherever
Harlequin books and ebooks are sold.

Harlequin.com

Get 4 FREE REWARDS!

We'll send you 2 FREE Books plus 2 FREE Mystery Gifts.

FREE
Value Over
$20

Both the **Harlequin Intrigue®** and **Harlequin® Romantic Suspense** series feature compelling novels filled with heart-racing action-packed romance that will keep you on the edge of your seat.